MW00464632

SEE HER RUN

(A Mia North FBI Suspense Thriller—Book 1)

Rylie Dark

Rylie Dark

Debut author Rylie Dark is author of the SADIE PRICE FBI SUSPENSE THRILLER series, comprising three books (and counting); the MIA NORTH FBI SUSPENSE THRILLER series, comprising three books (and counting); and the CARLY SEE FBI SUSPENSE THRILLER, comprising three books (and counting).

An avid reader and lifelong fan of the mystery and thriller genres, Rylie loves to hear from you, so please feel free to visit www.ryliedark.com to learn more and stay in touch.

BOOKS BY RYLIE DARK

SADIE PRICE FBI SUSPENSE THRILLER
ONLY MURDER (Book #1)
ONLY RAGE (Book #2)
ONLY HIS (Book #3)

MIA NORTH FBI SUSPENSE THRILLER
SEE HER RUN (Book #1)
SEE HER HIDE (Book #2)
SEE HER SCREAM (Book #3)

CARLY SEE FBI SUSPENSE THRILLER
NO WAY OUT (Book #1)
NO WAY BACK (Book #2)
NO WAY HOME (Book #3)

CHAPTER ONE

This is it.

Leaning forward in the front seat of the fed-issued Camry, Mia North watched the town car she'd been following for the past hour slow to a stop in front of a graffiti-covered Save-All mini-mart.

Keeping her distance, she eased into an empty five-dollar parking lot across the street, hoping the guy who took her money wouldn't also take her hubcaps. Then, keeping the wipers going to ward off the driving rain, she watched through the windshield and twisted the faux pearl ring on her pinky, waiting for something to happen.

The windows of the town car were black, so she could see no motion inside. No one stepped out. At least, not at first. The line-up of assorted riff-raff outside the market — there to deal drugs or turn tricks or whatever they did in broken neighborhoods like this — watched intently, because there was only one reason a car like that would be in downtown Dallas after dark.

And it wasn't anything good.

Mia heaved in a breath, then another, then reached over and unwrapped a piece of spearmint gum, feeding it into her mouth to calm her nerves.

She offered the sleeve to her partner, David, but he shook his head. "You know, if you're wrong about this, Pembroke's going to have your ass."

That was true. Luckily, Agent Pembroke had a soft spot for her. At least, she thought so. Not that the hard-ass would ever say so, but the results didn't lie. Because of her tenacity, Mia was well-known as one of the best in the Dallas-Fort Worth field office, so she'd earned it. Tough as a bulldog to most of the agents on the force, he gave her a little leeway.

But even Mia had to admit that this hunch was going *way* outside the realm of what was safe.

When they'd set out to track the man out of his high-rise apartment in ritzy Highland Park, she'd hoped this would be an easy thing. She'd

1

hoped she'd be able to get some more damning evidence to add to her pile, and be done with this gig by dinner.

That was what she'd *hoped*. And what she hoped never aligned with what actually happened.

Because this was just too good. Too good to give up.

Once again, she found herself, thinking of her eight-year-old daughter, Kelsey, jumping into bed, without her mother to kiss her goodnight.

But this little jaunt to Cedar Crest? She *had* to be onto something. Looking around at the garbage-strewn streets and empty storefronts, all she knew was that this neighborhood was likely where dreams went to die. No ordinary up-and-coming politician would campaign on this crime-ridden street on a Saturday evening; but clearly, Wilson Andrews was anything but ordinary.

They watched as a prostitute — she had to be a prostitute, wearing a skin-tight dress that barely covered her butt — approached the suspect's car. The window powered down.

"That's all this is? He just wants some play?" David muttered. "Great. Waste of a Saturday."

"No . . .," Mia said, though of course, something like a soliciting charge would be damaging enough to the budding politician's career. But her hunch hadn't had anything to do with that. "I don't think that's what this is."

As expected, the prostitute just shrugged and stepped away from the car, a disappointed look on her face.

"This is going nowhere, *slow*," David muttered, checking his phone. "What is taking him so long? If he's going to do something, I wish he'd do it. I'm missing Frank's first game."

Two years ago, before he'd gotten the call to the show and attended Quantico, David had been a high school math teacher, and was used to things happening on a schedule. But after ten years on the force, Mia knew one thing: the FBI was *not* about keeping schedules.

"Just give it some time."

He heaved a sigh.

She glanced at the clock on her dash and gave him a sympathetic look. Their kids were about the same age, and Frank was playing first base this year. David, a single dad whose son was his life, had been so *proud*.

The urge to go home and call it a day was a powerful one, but she was so sure she was on the right track, this time. "Wait. Just wait. A couple more minutes. I promise."

David opened his mouth to yawn when the car's door opened. Mia nudged him, hard.

Her partner sat up like he had a rod up his ass as Wilson Andrews appeared. His thick, graying hair was perfectly coiffed and his three-piece suit without a wrinkle, like he was planning on delivering a speech to a bunch of dignitaries.

That's just what he had been doing, earlier that day. He was Number One with a Bullet to be the nominee for State Senate. People just *loved* Wilson Andrews, baby-kisser and promise-maker extraordinaire.

Unfortunately, his many fans and admirers didn't realize what a sleazebag he was. And that had nothing to do with his refusal to sponsor the bill that had given free healthcare to kids.

No, as Mia intended to prove, it went *way* past normal politician sleaze.

David, who wasn't exactly Calvin Klein and owned precisely one pair of jeans that he wore incessantly, stared in disgust. "Geez. Think the man ever wears anything that isn't a suit?"

"He has a reputation to uphold," she murmured, watching him.

He *did* stick out like a sore thumb, here. But perhaps he no longer cared. He'd allegedly done plenty of wrong, gotten implicated in tons of shady business, and had never so much as gotten a slap on the wrist. Now, he likely thought he was invincible. Famous billionaires with friends in high places, the Andrews clan was royalty around here, as invincible as the Kennedys and the Clintons.

Exactly why, when he took those underage girls, he thought he could get away with it.

Well, he *allegedly* took those girls. Mia happened to be the only one who alleged it, though. But in her head, she more than alleged. She *knew*.

Thus, him skulking around like a criminal. He had "No Good" written all over him. Wilson Andrews the Third looked around, and then went to his trunk, which he opened. He started to pull out some plastic Target bags, then, loading it all up into his arms, jogged across the street, toward their car.

They slinked down as he passed. "Where is he off to? You really think he kidnapped those girls?"

She nodded. *Definitely*. She had the evidence, mounds of it—logs indicating late-night phone calls, bizarre internet searches. Not to mention that Sara was the sixteen-year-old daughter of his old chum and roommate at Rice. She'd disappeared one morning, on her way to school. Then, two weeks later, her classmate and best friend, Chloe Braxton, had gone missing, too. With no witnesses and few leads, the case had gone cold, up until Mia had decided to check into it.

And all roads led to one man. As she went through the piles and piles of evidence the local police jurisdiction had collected, she noticed that one name kept coming up. Wilson Andrews. As busy as he was, *he'd* organized the search parties to find her. *He'd* offered a reward for her safe return. And according to interviews with the mother, prior to her disappearance, he'd been almost unnaturally close to the girl, offering her rides to school and the like. It had sent off all kinds of alarm bells in Mia's head.

She could see it, perfectly: He'd pursued her. Maybe offered her a ride to school. Got a little handsy with her. She'd fought him. Then she'd worried him, told him she was going to tell on him.

He couldn't allow that. So he did what he had to do.

Unfortunately, no one else in the precinct had believed Mia, despite the six previous cold cases she'd cracked over her nine years on the FBI. Wilson Andrews, it seemed, had powerful friends. No one wanted to touch him.

So Mia had done what *she* had to do. She'd kept quiet, biding her time, keeping tabs on him, collecting little bits of info to add to his file, but now . . .

Now, it was go-time.

Mixing with her adrenaline, the gum in her mouth tasted bitter. She spit it into the wrapper and flicked it into the cup holder. Once Andrews had gotten a sufficient distance away from her car, she opened her door and climbed outside, shivering in the thin drizzle.

"Hurry," she murmured to David, heading after their target.

David hefted his bodybuilder's frame out from the passenger seat and lumbered to stand next to her. As she crossed the parking lot, she saw their target duck inside a hole in a chain-link fence, disappearing between two boarded-up brick buildings. All the while, he scanned his surroundings, as if he was afraid someone would see him.

4

It looked like exactly what she'd simultaneously hoped for and dreaded... like he was up to the terrible things she suspected him of.

She brushed her hand along the butt of her gun at her ribcage. Feeling it there gave her a sense of security. Picking up her pace, she hurried after him as he rushed through the dark, narrow alley, strewn with and smelling of garbage. Her shoes were quickly ruined by puddles of muddy water.

When the alley opened up into a square courtyard, she looked around, confused. No. She couldn't have lost him. Not after all this.

She turned back, exasperated, to her young partner. "Where did he—"

A gunshot went off. Nearby. She could hear it, burrowing into the frame of the wooden shed next to her.

Mia dove to the ground for cover. *Someone is shooting at me.*

Frantic, she looked up, trying to decide where it'd come from. But night was beginning to fall, a thin mist settling over the barren yard. Everything was cloaked in darkness.

"There!" David shouted, and took off after him.

She raced after him, trying to overtake him. Not too difficult, since he was built for strength, not speed. She'd be pissed if, after all the work she did, *David* wound up taking him down.

She rounded a corner, well ahead of David, and found herself in a narrow alley, with a straight shot for the man as he raced for a chain link fence. No way out.

She had him.

Without stopping, she fisted the handle of her Glock, lifting it from her shoulder holster.

"FBI! Freeze!" Mia shouted, pointing it at the politician.

He did as she said, easily, almost too easily. He turned, holding up his hands—empty hands, with no gun in sight, and smiling an unsettling smile. The bastard was probably already thinking of what calls he'd make to get himself out of this mess. The Chief of Police. The Governor. They were all his best buds. Or maybe even a member of his rich family. There had to be some sleazy lawyers connected in there. If she hauled Andrews in now, without solid evidence, there was a very good chance he'd be back on the streets later tonight.

"What are you doing out here, Andrews?" she barked, carefully stepping closer on a ground covered with ruts from bicycles and patches of weeds.

5

"I don't think I need to answer that, Agent," he said placidly. "It's none of your business."

"Oh, it *is* my business. You were shooting at us. Evading us. And you're carrying . . ." She kicked a foot through the bags at his feet. "Bleach, duct tape, plastic bags . . . *Right*, you're just out for a stroll."

He snorted, amused. "First of all, I didn't shoot at you. Someone else did. This is not the best section of town, unfortunately." He sighed, "You can pat me down. No weapon. And secondly, your partner came at me in the dark, and didn't announce himself. I had no idea who he was. You blame me for running from Conan over there? He's a beast."

She narrowed her eyes at him. The man was smooth, with an oiliness that only made her more suspicious. This scumbag had a twelve-point lead in the polls? The voting public had to have been blind for him to have risen in the ranks as quickly as he had. She was done with his excuses. "Where are Sara Waverly and Chloe Braxton?"

His eyes went wide in mock indignation. She'd spent enough time studying his profile to know he was an accomplished actor. He'd even been part of the actors' guild at Rice. No one could believe a single thing he said or did. "How am I supposed to know?"

She kicked the bag and bit out every word: "Tell me where they are."

"If you must know, I bought a place in this area. I'm renovating it."

"You bought a place in Cedar Crest?" David asked doubtfully.

Andrews nodded.

Bullshit. His meter was off-the-charts. This wasn't exactly the neighborhood for a summer home, or even a rental unit. Due to the rash of crime, home values around here were going nowhere, fast. "What's the address?"

"Forty-seven Prescott."

"I'm checking it out."

He shrugged. "Of course. I wouldn't expect you to take my word for it."

She had no choice. Maybe, just maybe, she'd find something to help her solve Sara's disappearance. She could only hope.

Even if she did find more clues to lead them to the location of Sara Waverly's body, she'd likely get a mouthful-- maybe even worse— from Special Agent in Charge Pembroke. But she was just doing her job. And maybe it was just a hunch or women's intuition, but what was right, was right. She'd been nearly brought to tears by the press

6

conference footage of Sara's poor parents, red-eyed and haunted, begging for the young girl's safe return. She knew, better than anyone, what they were going through.

This sleaze deserved to be behind bars, and not just because of poor Sara.

Grabbing her cuffs, she barked, "Turn around. Put your hands behind your back."

He complied as if he'd done it a thousand times before, still effortlessly composed. "You're going to be sorry for this, Agent North."

So he knew her name. If her hunch turned out to be wrong, she'd probably never live it down. She could just imagine Wilson Andrews, speaking ill of her, a decade from now, from his desk in the Oval Office.

She decided not to cuff him yet.

"Go." She nudged him. "Show me this place."

He gave her an insolent shrug and headed the way they'd come. Occasionally, he seemed to be dragging his feet. She looked over at David, whose face seemed to say, *This has "bad idea" written all over it.*

"Trust me," she whispered to him, though at that moment, she wasn't sure she could trust herself.

On Broad Street, it was more of the same. A pawn shop with barred windows. More strewn garbage than garbage cans. Syringes in the gutters. A motley assemblage of unsmiling, tough-looking thugs hanging out on their front stoops, smoking and drinking beer. The moment the two agents and the politician appeared on the street, every eye was on them. "Right up this way, Agent," Andrews said pleasantly, as if he were a realtor, showing the place.

They turned another corner, onto a narrow side street called Prescott. If Mia hadn't had David with her, she'd have worried. She'd made it through tough scrapes before with just her Glock, prided herself on needing no man, but she was barely over five-foot-three and slim. This wasn't exactly the safest prospect.

He stopped at a burned-out shell of a brick building that even squatters would've found unsuitable. Every window was boarded up. The mossy stoop crumbled a bit beneath her feet as she climbed to a patch of black mold where a welcome mat once stood.

David laughed bitterly. "You could've really done *wonders* with this place with that gallon of bleach, man."

Mia's pulse skittered, and she only became more convinced she was on the right track. David was right. Bleach was like putting a Band-Aid on cancer. No amount of restoration would save this place. It was a hazard. It needed to be leveled.

Even so, the door seemed to be intact. Andrews produced a key, as if what was inside needed to be protected, and worked at the door. As he did, a couple of men in hoodies jumped off the stoop across the street and advanced toward them. "Yo, what are you doing over there, man?"

That could be trouble. David, though, had grown up in a neighborhood like this. He crossed his arms and gave them a look that said, *Stand down*. He knew better than to flash his badge, here.

It seemed to work. The men hesitated there, gauging the situation.

"Ah," Andrews said with a shrug. "Looks like I got the wrong key."

David snorted. "Right. I may have been born at night, but I wasn't born *last* night." He nudged forward. "Give it here."

Meanwhile, the men behind them continued to hoot and holler, even if they weren't coming any closer. Mia glanced over her shoulder as David fumbled with the key. No dice.

Mia let out a heavy sigh and backed away. Before, it had just been noise, something she ignored as easily as the catcalls she sometimes got. But at that moment, she actually listened to what the men across the street were saying. "Yo, man. Ain't you in the wrong place? This here's your place."

She looked across the street, at a house that made the one they were standing in front of look like the best of the Three Little Pigs' homes. Maybe in the Great Depression era, the clapboard shack had been a source of pride, but now, it was in the process of disintegrating into the earth beneath it. Its roof—and in fact, all of its lines—seemed to slant in unnatural ways, as if it was already in the process of being swallowed.

Her eyes rose to meet Andrews. He stood there, frozen, his Adam's apple bobbing in his throat. "If you let me go back to my car—"

She nudged David, who was still twisting the key in different directions, trying to get it to work. When he looked at her, she pointed across the street. *That's* the house.

"Huh?"

She grabbed the key and marched across the street. "Excuse me, gentlemen," she said to the men, who parted to let her pass.

No surprise, the key fit.

Andrews swallowed as she pushed open the door. "All these old houses look the same," he said, that swagger gone as he mustered a shrug.

Mia stepped into the darkened room, sure the first step would be a trap door. David and Andrews followed, the latter with his head down, mumbling to himself.

I've got him, she thought, ignoring the men once again, who were now shouting at them. Something about how this was their turf and outsiders weren't welcome here.

When the three of them were inside, Mia directed David to close the door and lock it. He did so, just in time, because the second the lock was in place, the hoods outside began to pound on the door.

But she had other things to concern herself with than being in the middle of a turf war.

She turned on the flashlight from her phone and arced it about the room. As she did, she saw movement. A couple of rats scurried along the baseboards of a room with a lumpy sofa, a threadbare oriental rug, and a battered player piano. Across the hall, a kitchen with peeling, charred wallpaper seemed to have been the source of a few too many cooking accidents. A staircase with a rather pretty bannister swept up to the second floor, but some of the wooden floorboards were missing.

The men outside were banging hard on the door, trying to get in, shouting obscenities. They were just looking for something to fill the time. Eventually, they'd give up and go away. She hoped. Right now, they didn't need any more trouble.

She went farther in, shining the light everywhere she could, hoping for some clue. She came to a door, opening it to find nothing more than a closet. There was an old bowling ball in the dark recesses of it, but nothing else.

Carefully, she climbed the stairs, the structure creaking beneath her. She found bedrooms with rotting mattresses and rusted bed frames, a bathroom with a massive clawfoot tub. Plenty of insects and cobwebs.

But nothing to indicate Sara or Chloe had ever been here.

Turning, she briefly caught sight of Andrews's smug smiled. "Satisfied?"

She shook her head, pacing the floor. Outside, the men were still knocking, making it nearly impossible for her to concentrate.

She wasn't satisfied. There had to be more than this. There just had to be.

"Is there a basement?"

Andrews shook his head. "No, and you're wasting your time. You're done, Agent. You're going to hear from my attorney, and they'll have your badge so fast—"

"Crawl space? Attic?" She studied the ceiling, which had holes in the drywall that bared the rafters up above. Nothing to indicate a door was or ever had been there.

"Nope. Not that I know of. Like I said, I've only owned the place--"

"All right." She made a mental note to check on the ownership records. Other than that, she was at a loss. *Not another dead end.*

The knocking continued.

Her hands shaking with desperation she snapped, "David. Can you get rid of those guys? I can't hear myself think."

"On it," he said, heading down the stairs.

She followed a moment later, exasperated. As she did, she found David at the foot of the stairs, staring wide-eyed at the ground. The knocking continued.

"David!" she muttered. "What's the problem? I told you to get rid of those guys."

He shook his head. "They're gone."

She paused, listening. No, the sound wasn't coming from the other side of the door, after all. It was coming from down below, under their feet. And it wasn't the sound of knuckles on wood. It was a metallic, clanging noise.

She spun on Andrews. "There's no crawl space?" she demanded.

For the first time, he looked rather nervous. He shrugged. "Well, I don't—"

But they'd already set out, looking for the door. Sure enough, Mia found it, underneath the rug in the living room. When she pulled open the latch, she shone her light upon a ladder that descended into a basement. There were footprints in the dirt below that looked like they belonged to a pair of dress loafers.

She had a very good idea who those belonged to.

"Holy—" David started, as the knocking became louder.

10

"Hey," Andrews said, his voice now an octave higher. When she shone the light across his face, his forehead glistened with new droplets of sweat. "I didn't even know that was—"

"Hold onto him," Mia instructed David, quickly taking the ladder down. "Make sure he doesn't go anywhere."

It was cooler below, and smelled like mold. The cinderblock walls of the basement were weeping. She arced her flashlight in all directions before stopping at what looked like a heap of blankets.

But then she realized it was a tangle of pale limbs and a web of blonde hair. The girl was gathered up in a corner, wrapped in a wool blanket and handcuffed to the piping there.

Though the waif in front of her was a shadow of the smiling yearbook photo she'd taped in her cubicle, she recognized the girl at once. "Chloe?"

Mia approached her, her heart thudding, afraid of what she might find. Was she . . . alive?

The movement wasn't just a trick of the eye. She was holding a metal cup, still rhythmically banging it against the pipe, her face dirty, her eyes unfocused, lower lip trembling.

Behind her, Andrews's voice was nothing like the one he used when addressing his constituents. "I didn't . . . I don't know . . . how did she . . .?"

"Save it," David barked, then breathed, "Jesus Christ."

"It's all right. You're safe now," Mia soothed, reaching out to smooth back the girl's hair. She whirled around, shining the light into all corners. No movement. Nothing. Her flashlight went to Andrews. "Where's the other girl? Where's Sara?"

He continued to shake his head blankly, blinking in the bright light as he professed his innocence.

But in the split second before she pulled the light away from his face, she could've sworn she saw the man smile.

CHAPTER TWO

One Week Later

"So, I want to hear everything about this case," Mia's older sister Francine said, leaning forward as they sipped their margaritas under the umbrella the following weekend. It was perfect weather for a barbecue, and because it was near to everyone, Mia's suburban University Park home always seemed to be the place for her family get-togethers. "Did they really let Andrews go, even after everything they found?"

Mia nodded, still feeling bitter about the whole thing. But she'd been on the force long enough to know that was sometimes how the cookie crumbled. "He's out on bail. But Pembroke thinks he'll get off."

Their mother groaned and primly sipped her margarita. "Oh, girls, do we have to talk business all the time?"

Francine was front-desk at the DFW Police, and though she heard her share of crime stories, this one was for the record books. She ignored their mother and whispered, "How is that even possible? Details!"

"They'll find some loophole, somewhere. You know how connected he is," she said with a sigh. "They decided there was no evidence to hold him there. But it's mostly because he has everyone in his back pocket, from the Chief of police to every judge on the circuit."

"But you basically caught him with his hand in the cookie jar."

Mia nodded. "But the house really did belong to him, as do five others on that block. He fixes them up and rents them out. His story checked out, and Chloe couldn't make a positive identification."

"And no Sara Waverly?"

"Nope." Mia stared deeply into the slush of her margarita. "He lawyered up right away, and he knows better than to talk. But it might be good. Considering Sara's still missing. There's a chance he could slip up and lead us to her, if she's still alive."

"Do you really believe that she's alive?"

"I don't know." She had to admit, it was doubtful. They'd found blood at the last place she was seen, and if she wasn't with Chloe? Mia had put together the likely story in her mind: Hoping to quell his

12

obsession with the young girl, Andrews had kidnapped and killed Sara. After disposing of her body, he found his hunger had only grown. Thus, Chloe.

Of course, without a body, there was still hope.

And Chloe had been found. That was a good thing.

"Has the other girl said anything else about what happened?"

"Chloe hasn't really spoken. She's experienced so much trauma." Mia glanced across their backyard, to where her eight-year-old daughter Kelsey was at the half-court in the back of their house, showing her grandfather how good she was getting in basketball by throwing layup after perfect layup. The last thing she wanted was for her inquisitive eight-year-old to be asking questions about the Sara and Chloe case.

For most parents, it was enough to shield their children from the news . . . but Mia had to shield her daughter from *life*. She was extra protective of her daughter, not just because of this latest kidnapping case, but even before then. Once, she'd noticed someone watching Kelsey at the bus stop. He'd sped away before she could approach him, but she'd always wondered . . .

A fleeting thought of Ellis Horvath touched her mind, but she shut it out.

Mia had enemies. And the last thing she wanted to do was to bring them home to her family.

"Who hasn't?" Francine mumbled, slurping down her drink.

Mia glanced over at their mother and then gave her sister a warning look. "She did say that her kidnapper wore a mask, so she couldn't identify him. Maybe if she remembers something in the future, that will change things. So I don't know if there's much to tell yet."

That was a lie. There was plenty to tell. The girls had been missing six months. The police had all but given up on the case a month ago, which was when Mia had come in. But in that time, the poor sixteen-year-old Chloe had been abused, beaten to a shadow of her old self. She'd likely always be haunted by the horrific events she'd been through, and who could blame her? She'd never again be that All-American, honor roll girl who had everything going for her. And who knew if she'd ever see her best friend again?

Mia hadn't been there for Andrews's interrogation—it had happened a couple of days ago—but in it, he'd refused to say anything but that he wanted to consult his lawyer, who'd promptly worked his magic and gotten him released.

But Mia could fill in the blanks. Andrews had made a pass at Sara Waverly while driving her to school, and she'd rebuffed him. He'd found the one thing in life he couldn't have. In a moment of madness, he'd decided to keep her as his own.

And then, typical of men like him, drunk on power, he'd decided that one wasn't enough. So he'd taken poor Chloe.

So where was Sara Waverly?

But this was not the time to discuss it. As much as Mia's family marinated in crime from day-to-day, child kidnappings were one thing they didn't discuss.

All because of Sam Jr.

It had happened over twenty years ago, but the wounds had never fully gone away. Mia only had to look at the three photographs on her parents' mantle at the home she'd grown up in—two of them, of Francie and herself, in their college caps and gowns. One of Sam, in the very center, with his lopsided bowl-shaped haircut and missing front-teeth, forever in kindergarten.

As strong as her parents were, they'd been helpless to do anything about that. And grief never took a vacation. Sometimes, it sneaked up on a person, at the most unexpected of times.

Mia cleared her throat and glanced at their mother, who was absently nursing her margarita.

"Right," Francine said, finally getting the hint and giving their mom a little hug. Then she swiped her white-blonde hair into a messy ponytail on the top of her head. "So, you're off for the weekend?"

She nodded. "Amazing, huh? It's rare we get to be all together."

Her mother tutted. "Poor Kelsey was telling me she can't remember the last time you picked her up from school."

Mia sighed. It was true. She'd been so busy—*obsessed* was probably more like it—with the Waverly case. And it felt like just a week ago that Kelsey was still in diapers. Now, she was growing so fast, all spindly, long legs. In no time, she'd be taller than Mia. "Well, I'm going to. Things have just been a bit busy . . ."

Wearing his *Grillmaster* apron, her husband Aidan came over with the first selection of burgers and dogs—perfectly grilled, of course. It was a good thing he worked from home, in IT, because he was always around whenever her crazy schedule took her away from the house. Not to mention, he was a great cook. She had no idea what she'd have done without him.

As if sensing how much the comment stung her, he leaned over and kissed the top of her head. She smiled up gratefully at him. They'd talked about having more kids, but Kelsey was a handful, on her own.

Mia scooped up the most perfect hot dog—Kelsey would complain if it was too burned—and placed it on a paper plate, slathering on ketchup. "Time to eat!" she called to them, putting a pickle on the side.

As she set it down at Kelsey's place and went to grab her own burger, her phone began to ring.

Aidan rolled his eyes. "There goes the weekend!"

It wasn't unusual for Mia to get calls at all hours of the day. And she never felt comfortable silencing her phone because what if it was important? But as she glanced at her phone, expecting to see PEMBROKE on the display, she frowned. It said *Unknown Number.*

Strange. The area code was 214. Dallas.

She snapped her fingers. "I know what this is. I bet Kelsey's new glasses are in."

"Really?" Kelsey clapped her hands. She'd been on pins and needles for her new prescription to come in. She'd ordered a pair of clear-framed Coach glasses, the most expensive and trendiest ones in the place. When Mia had been a kid, she had no clue what Coach even was. But she'd given in, because she'd already been the Bad Mom, turning her daughter down for contacts.

She answered, expecting to hear the pleasant voice informing her that her order was ready for pick-up.

"Agent North? Agent Mia North?" the voice sounded soft, faraway, tremulous.

Mia's spine straightened. The voice was eerily like Chloe's that night when she'd finally spoken. All she'd said was, *I want to go home,* but it was so heart-wrenching and childlike; it was a sound Mia knew she'd never forget.

So was this . . .

"Yes? Who is this?"

At the warning tone in Mia's voice, everyone around the table turned and looked at her. She stood up and walked into the house, certain something was wrong. She waited for an answer, but all she heard was more, desperate crying.

Mia gasped out, "Sara?"

"Ye-es," the female voice said, sobbing, hysterical. "Please. I need you here. I need your help."

"All right. Where?"

"Fifty-nine Weston."

Heart thumping, she ran inside, looking around for her car keys, when the full weight of the woman's words hit her. *"Fifty-nine Weston?"*

It was an address she knew well, all because of one person. Ellis Horvath. This was his neighborhood.

A tendril of fear gripped her as the person on the other end said, "Yes! Please! He says to come alone! He's going to kill me!"

Locating her purse, grabbing her keys and unlocking the gun cabinet, she said, "Okay. Hold on. I'm coming. I'll be right there."

She ended the call, grabbed her Glock, and turned to find her husband, staring at her, concern etched in his features. "I take it you're going to need that burger to-go?"

She barely registered the question as she gave him a quick kiss and reached for the door to the garage. The adrenaline was now pumping through her veins. "No time. I'll be back soon," she said, then added, once she'd closed the door and was out of earshot, "I hope."

CHAPTER THREE

Oh, my God. It had never occurred to her before, but now, it seemed obvious. Was it possible she'd been wrong all along about Wilson Andrews? That his knowing the Waverly family was just a coincidence? That someone else was responsible, instead?

"David. Listen to me," Mia said into her speakerphone as she floored the gas pedal to make it through an intersection before the light turned red.

He groaned. "You always find a way to brighten up my weekends," he mumbled.

True. That's why he was Number Two on her speed-dial, just after Aidan. "Listen. Are you listening?"

"Yeah. Talk."

"Call nine-one-one. Tell the police to meet us around the corner from fifty-nine Weston. Tell them you have reason to believe Sara Waverly is there. *Now.*"

His response wasn't much different to hers. "Whoa. What? Why? Why does that address sound fam—"

"Ellis Horvath."

"Right." He whistled. "Shit. Are you telling me—"

"I'll tell you more when you get here. Just do it. Text me when you're on your way. All right?"

"Sure. On it."

She ended the call, put an elbow on the door, and massaged the start of a headache away from her temple. Her every muscle was tight, zinging with tension, a tension that wasn't going away anytime soon.

Ellis Horvath.

The name often made her bite her tongue until she tasted blood. One of the first cases she'd worked on with David, Ellis Horvath had been a science teacher who was also a pedophile. He was accused of murdering one of his students, a twelve-year old Ashley Lopez. The only thing they'd had to go on was hundreds of pornographic images that had been taken from his computer, and an eye-witness account that

17

placed someone of Horvath's physical description on the path near the park where the body of the child was found.

Horvath didn't deny that he'd been in the park—he ran there every day, he said. But there was no physical evidence tying him to the little girl's death, and so he'd been charged for the pornography and served only two years.

But the damage had been done. Horvath had lost everything—his job, his family, his livelihood.

And he'd blamed it on Mia North.

She'd been there for his sentencing. When the two-year sentence for possession of child pornography was handed down, he looked straight at her and mouthed, *I'm going to get you, bitch. You and your daughter.*

Mia shivered at the thought. She'd dealt with plenty of cold-hearted criminals in her time, but none had threatened Kelsey so blatantly. And now that Kelsey was about the same age as Ashley Lopez, she couldn't help making the connection . . .

After his release, weird things had begun to happen. At first, she'd thought she was being paranoid. But then Kelsey had reported seeing a "weird man" following her.

Every time Mia thought about that car, speeding away from Kelsey's bus stop, she imagined it was Ellis Horvath. Every time she heard a sound outside, she imagined his face, peeking in her window.

She couldn't tell Ellis Horvath that he had damaged his *own* life . . . now, he seemed hell-bent on damaging hers and those of the people she loved, too. Sometimes she thought he was only biding his time. Was it possible that he had something to do with the Waverly case, too? Theories teemed in her head, but she couldn't seem to make the connection. How were these two cases related?

By the time Mia made it to downtown Dallas, a thin drizzle had begun to fall. As she pulled up at the curb, she squinted past the raindrops on the windshield, and a shiver went down her spine. Fifty-nine Weston was beside an overgrown field, littered with discarded tires, rusting oil drums, the carcasses of long-expired automobiles and decaying railroad ties. There was a faded sign painted upon the brick façade of the building, over the door: *Fanciful Ribbon Company, EST 1912.*

Apparently, Fanciful Ribbon hadn't been in operation for a long time. The front of the place was crisscrossed with graffiti-emblazoned wooden boards. No windows except for on the top floor, and those were dark. It looked like an abandoned warehouse below, some apartments on the second floor.

The back of her neck tingled. She let her breath out slowly. She stepped out over a puddle, quickly crossed the sidewalk and pulled on the door handle, not expecting it to budge. To her surprise, it creaked open. She slipped it open a few inches and saw nothing but darkness.

She reached into her pocket and pulled out her cell phone to use as a flashlight. The building was an old manufacturing plant. The door entered into a small waiting room, with a spider-webbed receptionist's window overlooking it. She treaded carefully across the peeling linoleum floor and opened the door opposite.

It led out to an expansive factory floor, full of hulking machinery from a bygone age. A gridwork of metal scaffolding hung several stories above, and the sheer size of the room made even the quiet, graceful steps of her shoes echo like a herd of thundering elephants. Pausing to listen, she heard only the sound of trickling water. Arcing the light from her phone across the expanse, she soon noticed the source of it. An enormous, swimming pool-sized puddle had formed in the center of the room, the result of a persistent leak from the ceiling above.

Mia shivered. She had the distinct impression that if someone was here, the element of surprise would not be on her side.

No, in fact, it felt like she was being watched.

Her phone in her hand buzzed with a text. It was from David. *On my way. Be there in fifteen.*

David always erred on the side of caution, so she knew that fifteen was likely ten. Still, it wasn't good enough. She couldn't wait.

She looked down and saw footprints in the dust. Wet footprints. The prints headed off toward an opening to another room.

Mia broke into a run and skirted the puddle, heading for the adjacent room. When she stopped abruptly, listening for any sound, she heard nothing but the steady drip of water.

"Hello?" she said, aloud this time, scanning the shapes of the machinery for any sign of life. "Ellis? Ellis Horvath?"

"*You,*" a voice boomed in the darkness, cutting through the silence like a blade.

She froze and dropped her phone, sending a beam of light errantly swirling about like a disco ball. When it came to rest on the ground, it illuminated the man who'd spoken to her for the briefest of instances. He was sitting in a chair, in the very corner of the vast room.

As she bent down to reach for it, scrabbling to pick up the phone, the voice came again: "Stay there."

By now, her eyes were adjusting to the minimal light. The man across the way was wearing glasses, his hair a little shaggy, but other than that, he was dressed in a business-casual way, with dockers and a button-down shirt. Good looking, respectable, and . . . someone she knew quite well.

It was Ellis Horvath.

He was holding something in his hand, half-obscured by shadows.

A gun?

Squinting, trying to grasp what was happening before her, she took a step backwards, her instincts telling her to reach for her sidearm.

"Don't do it. Don't even move."

"Horvath?" she shouted, her voice echoing hollowly through the vast warehouse. "If you have Sara Waverly here, tell me where she is. No one has to get--"

"Don't talk, bitch."

His voice sounded strange. Harder than she remembered, almost otherworldly, like it was coming from everywhere, echoing around the entire expanse of the warehouse.

She didn't need him to answer. She knew exactly what he was doing. Getting his revenge, once and for all.

Suddenly, a gunshot went off, the sound blasting her eardrums. She ducked instinctively. The sound seemed to ricochet wildly about the room, bouncing off walls around her.

She lunged forward to grab him, pulling him to the ground. He lifted his gun to her and fumbled on the trigger. Pushing his hand to the side, Mia fisted her hand around the handle of her gun and yanked it from her holster as she lost her grip on Ellis's arm. She hit the ground and aimed seconds later, firing off one round.

There came a sickeningly wet, guttural sound as her bullet found its mark. Grabbing her phone, she aimed the light at her target. A flower of bright red blood was blooming at his chest.

She stared at it, trying to comprehend, then looked at Horvath's eyes, which were rolling back into his head. She dipped a hand under his neck, feeling for a pulse, but there was nothing. His head lolled. He was still warm, but dead.

20

She'd killed him.

Heart thudding, she looked around, trying to make sense of this. Arcing the light every which way, she strained to see his victim. But there was no Sara Waverly.

She was alone.

CHAPTER FOUR

An hour later, Mia sat in an overly-air-conditioned metal interrogation room in the downtown detention center, twisting the faux pearl ring on her pinky and waiting for Special Agent in Charge Warren Pembroke to arrive.

Warren Pembroke. *The man.*

Tall and strong and stoic, she'd never, in all her years in the agency, seen him crack a smile. He was the type to induce shivers in all who crossed him. But right now, she needed him. He'd always had a soft spot for her. He'd help her sort all this out.

Instead, when the door opened, a slim man in a plaid, button-down shirt and khakis walked in. He had his detective badge, displayed proudly on his belt. "Hello, Agent North. I'm Detective Reynolds, from the Dallas PD."

She blinked as the fluorescent light shone down on her, illuminating her clothes, still covered in a splatter of blood from Ellis Horvath. It'd never felt so harsh, so blinding before. Other than that, there was nothing other than a video camera, likely recording this whole exchange.

She twisted the ring more. She'd never been on *this* side of the table before. "Hi."

Mia expected he'd say something about her sister. Everyone knew Francine North, because she'd been on the force for a long time and was the smiling face behind the desk at the main precinct. Or maybe even her father. Her father's career was long and distinguished. There was a picture of him in the hallway, outside this very room.

But he didn't say any of that. He didn't even offer her a hand to shake. He laced his fingers into a ball on the cold table between them. His voice was deep, monotone, the pad in front of him as empty as Mia's mind.

No. Actually, her mind was *full.* So full of swirling thoughts, not one of them made sense.

When they'd arrived downtown, she expected someone would buy her a cup of coffee to calm her nerves. Instead, no one looked her in the eye as they brought her in. She'd been shuttled in here unceremoniously, like a . . .

Like a criminal?

No. That wasn't it. Ellis Horvath may have been an ex-con, but he was still a total dirtbag. And he was dead. He deserved it, after what he'd done. She'd had every reason to defend herself. This was just procedure. Any time there was a murder, heads rolled. They were probably just doing due diligence to wrap things up.

He pressed a button on the digital recorder between them.

"This is Kevin Reynolds. I'm here with Agent Mia North regarding the events of earlier tonight, August twelve. Agent North, can you please tell me what happened, in your own words."

She nodded. She'd gone over the details, ad nauseum, to the police officers who responded to her call, then the agents, and then Reynolds himself. But if she'd learned anything from Francine, who'd been with the force for years, it was that the Dallas Police Department was a stickler for the rules. They had to get everything on record.

Smoothing the bandage on her forehead, she sat up a little taller and said, "I received a phone call from an unknown number, from someone—someone who identified herself as Sara Waverly—saying she was being held by a man and needed me to come quickly to fifty-nine Weston. I went there, and that was when I saw Ellis Horvath. He had a gun. We fought, a gunshot went off, and I returned fire, killing Horvath. That's all."

Reynolds nodded. "You were lucky to get out of there with only that." He pointed to her forehead.

She didn't feel lucky. Her fingers shook so much that she had to lace her hands together, tightly, in her lap. She just wanted to go home and sleep. If she could. In all her years on the force, she'd never had to shoot anyone. Ellis Horvath may have been a scumbag but ending anyone's life was not to be taken lightly. She never wanted to have to do that again. "I suppose."

"The victim . . .," he went on.

The victim. It took her a moment to realize he was speaking of Horvath. For the past year, *she'd* felt like a victim. When she saw that car, slowly idling by Kelsey's bus stop. When she answered the phone to nothing but dead air. Whenever her family went anywhere without her. "What about him?"

"You two have had quite a history."

She shook her head. "I helped gather the evidence so he could be arrested, yes, for the murder of Ashley Lopez."

Reynolds nodded as he flipped through his papers. "Right. The twelve-year-old girl in his science class at Dallas Middle School."

Mia nodded. "But he was let go. They didn't think it was enough to convict him."

"And it's a crime that, to this day, he swears he didn't commit."

She snorted. "Despite the fact that he had scores of child porn on his home computer."

"That doesn't make him a murderer."

Mia scrubbed her hands down her face. "Sara Waverly called me and told me that he was going to kill her and I needed to get to fifty-nine Weston, which is Horvath's address."

"Above the ribbon factory."

She nodded.

"Run me though it one more time . . .," he said, to which Mia groaned inwardly. How many times did she have to go over this? "What, exactly, did this girl say?"

"She said that he was going to kill her. She sounded really distraught."

"How did you know it was Sara Waverly?"

She shrugged. "I don't know. I asked, and she said—"

"You asked?"

"Yes. I mean, I think I did. I just . . . I guess I . . ."

"Assumed?"

She stared at him, hard. She couldn't remember. Had she asked? Everything was jumbled in her head. "No . . ." *Well, maybe.*

"And when you got there?"

"I went inside the warehouse. The door was open. I was looking for the steps up to the apartments, because I've been there before, but it was dark. But he was standing in a corner. He told me not to move. And then . . ."

She gnawed on the side of her cheek, remembering those tense moments.

"And then?"

"We wrestled. He shot at me. I don't know. And the response was me, acting in defense."

24

She swallowed. *And right then was probably when he died.* She'd gotten him right in the heart. A clean shot. She hadn't been first in her class in firearms training at Quantico for nothing.

"As for your history . . ."

She *really* could've used that coffee. Even the crappy drip stuff they served up in the kitchenette would be fine. Or a ride home. That would've been better. She checked her phone and said, "Did you guys check that place thoroughly? Because I could've sworn I heard a girl's voice, and—"

Reynolds spoke over her. "Look. I'll tell you what we found, Agent, and you can tell us what we're supposed to think," he said, setting his hands back on the cold steel table. He sat up taller and broadened his massive shoulders, becoming even more formidable.

Mia swallowed. *Where, exactly, is he going with this?*

"We looked through the scene and at Ellis Horvath's body, and we have your word that you shot him." His eyes met hers. "And we have an entire agency who knows how pissed off you were when he was released from prison." His eyes darkened as he added, "Some would say you were *obsessed.*"

Mia impulsively sat back in her seat, creating distance between them. All she could think was, *He's not going* there, *is he?* "He stalked my daughter, Reynolds. I saw him, at my daughter's bus stop. I think--" She swallowed as she remembered what Aidan had said—*You're probably just imagining things.* "I think I saw him in my yard."

"Or so you say."

She gritted her teeth. That was the consensus, these days. That she was paranoid. "I *know.*"

"But no one else seems to know that. No one else saw him. What we do know is that you took the news of Horvath's release hard."

"I didn't take his release hard. What I did take hard is when he decided to take revenge on me for apprehending him in the first place. The pornography charge might be the only one that stuck, but that's not all he's done. He deserves to be in jail!" she said, incredulous. "If you're trying to accuse me of some vigilante justice, that's ridiculous! I've been on this force for nine years and have yet to have even a smudge on my record. You know th—"

"I've never seen anyone take a case so hard before, North. You were becoming unhinged. You were—"

"Unhinged? No. Concerned. The bastard was *stalking* us. And no one seemed to care."

Reynolds snapped his notebook shut, let out a guttural grunt and stood. "Wait here."

"Wait!" Mia slammed her fist on the table. The abrupt explosion of flesh to metal made Reynolds raise an eyebrow. That was the extent of his surprise.

He didn't wait. He strode out the door, leaving her desperately alone. She thought of Kelsey, lying in bed without another goodnight kiss from her mom. She thought of Aidan, managing all the motherly duties quite well, the saint that he was. She thought of Sara Waverly and Chloe Braxton and all the other child victims of terrible adults, who were never going to live a normal life, and of Ellis Horvath, who'd never have a chance to pay for his horrible crimes. But most of all, she wondered what was going to happen, now, to her.

She didn't have to wonder for long. Another agent came in and, grim-faced, said, "Mia North, you are under arrest for the murder of Ellis Horvath . . ."

She stared at the man as he clipped the handcuffs on, the words of the Miranda rights blurring together, monotone. Words she'd heard a thousand times but never directed at her. Eventually, they were replaced by the sound of her own heartbeat, thundering in her ears.

The walk of shame down the hallway to the jail cell was a blur. She was vaguely aware of other officers in the detention center, watching her, agog. Most of the time, though, Mia kept her eyes on the ground, sure that at any moment, she'd wake up from this nightmare. Or that David would run in and tell her this was all a joke, or that *Whoops, we made a mistake. Your record is impeccable, Agent. Of course, you couldn't have done this thing.*

Nothing like that happened. Instead, she wound up on the bottom bunk of a bed in a cold jail cell in the precinct, listening to one of the guards, who was playing "Gangnam Style" on repeat, probably trying to drive all the inmates insane.

The mattress was about an inch thick. There was a toilet, right across from her. The cell on the other side of the hall was empty, but even so, she decided she'd *really* have to go before she just dropped her pants in the middle of things and went.

Besides, very soon, they'd all realize they made some terrible error of judgement, and let her free.

She kept looking up at the door, every time a guard passed, waiting for that to happen.

The more she did, the more her hands shook. Eventually, she had to sit on them. *I won Agent of the Month last June. Pembroke congratulated me personally. Took me to lunch. I have the plaque in my office,* she reminded herself. *This is not happening. Not to me.*

But the glory of that moment shattered every time she looked around at her current surroundings.

As the night wore on, she became so tired, she wound up lying on the stained pillow at the foot of the bed, wondering what was taking them so long. The least someone could do was let her call her family to tell them what was going on. Instead, when they'd arrested her, they'd taken all her personal items. Her gun, her phone. Now, she felt naked. Unprotected.

Scared.

She'd almost nodded off when she heard a sound of metal upon metal, key in a lock.

She looked up to find the guard opening the door for her. Special Agent in Charge Pembroke was there.

Mia leaped up, relieved. "Oh, thank God. You've told them this is all a mistake?"

He held up his hands, then looked around the place in disgust. Crossing his arms, he said, "Is it?"

That was not the response she'd wanted to hear.

"Of course!" she shouted in shock, hardly able to believe he'd ask that. "Of course it is. I don't belong here. Someone needs to—"

"It's not that simple. I'm doing everything I can. All right? You're gonna have to sit tight and let this thing get played out."

Played out? She looked around the cell. This was ridiculous. Couldn't they see? "But—"

"No, listen to me. By all appearances, it looks like you went to Horvath's place of residence and entered without permission to—"

"It was open. It was an abandoned ware—" Her vocal cords froze when he gave her that icy look. It suddenly struck her just why it was open.

It was an invitation. To her own execution.

"People are saying it looks like you have a vendetta against him."

Her eyes narrowed. "So I hear. Who is saying that, besides Reynolds?"

He didn't respond.

"But what about the phone call?"

"It came from Horvath's cell phone. And we don't have any record of what was said."

"Someone could've rerouted it. Someone who wanted to make it look like it was him, because--"

"Who would want to do that?"

She stared at him. Maybe he was just playing the devil's advocate, but if Pembroke didn't believe her, the situation felt hopeless. "I can't believe they're doing this. Someone—someone set me up, sir."

He nodded. "It looks that way. And I'm sorry this happened to you, Mia. But right now, the prosecution is piling up an awful lot of evidence against you."

"Right, but it's all bullshit."

"I hope that it is."

She frowned and studied him. He hadn't yet told her that he believed she was innocent. And right now, she really needed to hear that. She had to know that after her nine years on the force, somebody here trusted her, had her back. "You should *know*. *You* know I was set up. *You* know I only killed him in self-defense. Right?"

He didn't answer. Instead, he pressed his lips together and gave a cursory glance around the cell. "Just sit tight and let the wheels of justice turn."

So that was a no. She let out a laugh of utter disbelief and threw up her hands. "I can't believe this. I can't believe this is happening to me."

"Look. I'm on your side, North. We're going to get you out of this, but there's a little web that's been woven, and it's going to take some time to cut through the strands."

She glanced at him. Nice try, but he *still* hadn't said he believed she hadn't killed Ellis Horvath on purpose.

"Okay," she said finally. "Can you tell me something? How is Chloe?"

He looked surprised that she would ask, then shook his head. "She's not good. Still in shock. Other than the first few hours when she said she couldn't identify her assailant because he was wearing a mask, she's not talking anymore. And we don't know if she ever will."

"Andrews did it," she mumbled. "It was his house. Check the deed. You'll see it's under his name."

"It is, but his family owns half the real estate in Cedar Crest. They—"

"But he had to have done it. No matter how slick they are, his lawyer can't—"

"Mia," he said, cutting her off.

"Yes?"

"You need to stop doing your job right now, and worry about yourself."

She nodded, sufficiently scolded. As hard as that was, he was right. If the prosecution was framing a case around her that said she was obsessive, it didn't look good for her case to act obsessive about any other case right now. "All right. Can I call my family?"

"I'll call your husband and let him know."

He nodded curtly at her and called for the guard to let him out.

When the cell door clanged shut, it did so with chilling finality. Looking around the cell, it felt smaller than ever. She'd be in front of the judge soon for the arraignment, but not now, in the late hours of evening. So that meant she'd be spending the night here.

She might as well get comfortable. If that was even possible.

CHAPTER FIVE

As expected, Mia didn't sleep. Not for one second.

So there was no time to forget where she was. She was aware of every painful moment of her night in that bleak jail cell. She heard water drip hollowly from the faucet in the rusty corner sink about twelve-thousand times. She smelled the foul odor of a guard's burned microwave popcorn. She heard the guards' dress shoes squeaking as they walked up and down the corridor. She heard the snores of a fellow inmate, even if she couldn't see him beyond the cinderblock walls that threatened to close in on her.

And in the morning, just as the first light of day was casting a gray gloom upon the walls, she decided she really had to pee.

Quickly, she went over and did her business. Then she went to the sink and splashed water on her face.

A lawyer. I forgot to ask Pembroke about a lawyer, she thought when she sat back down on the creaking bed. She went through her mental list of friends that she could call in a favor from. Plenty of cops—she came from a long line of those. But no criminal defense lawyers. In fact, she'd pissed off plenty of attorneys in her career, trying to cajole their clients into revealing their guilt. Aidan didn't know anyone either.

Aidan. Her heart squeezed at the thought of his reaction when he'd gotten the call last night from Pembroke. Kelsey, too.

What if she was found guilty? What if she was sentenced to prison for years and missed Kelsey's childhood entirely?

Pushing those thoughts away, she stood up and paced, trying to energize herself into thinking clearly. No, this wasn't as bad as it looked. It was a mistake. She didn't need a lawyer. If they didn't have enough evidence to convict someone like Ellis Horvath for murder, the same could be said about her. This was an open and shut case. The judge would have to see it.

Not only that, but it's a lie. Someone's not telling the truth, because I'm innocent. So we just have to find out who is setting me up. That's all.

30

But who?

Relax, Mia. Stop putting the cart before the horse. Just worry about getting out of here, first. Then you can figure out the rest of it.

Slowly, the minutes ticked by. Just when she thought she'd been forgotten, a black female guard came by, holding a tray of breakfast. "Wake up, agent," she said pleasantly, turning her key in the lock. "Eat up. You've got a big day ahead of you."

The tray had a pint of milk and some bran flakes on it, as well as some sad looking grapes and a carton of OJ, but Mia wasn't hungry. She didn't touch it when the guard set it on the bed in front of her.

"Big day . . .?"

"You're first, lucky girl. Nine o'clock arraignment."

She stood up. That was weird. Were they fast-tracking the case? "What time is it now?"

The woman backed away and pointed at the tray. "Eat. We'll come get you."

Mia didn't touch the tray. She sat on the edge of the bed, counting the moments until the door jangled open again. This time, a male guard motioned for her to turn around. She did, and he snapped on her handcuffs, then led her out into the hallway.

Again, the walk of shame, but this time, she knew where they were headed. Down the corridor and across the breezeway to the county courthouse.

There was no one in the hall, which was why it came as a surprise when the door to the breezeway opened and a photographer snapped her picture. She blinked as the officer escorting her said, "Get out of here; what are you doing in here?" He continued to snap photos as another officer guided him away.

A sick feeling swelled in Mia's gut. Would those pictures show up in the newspaper? Would Kelsey see them?

The vast courtroom was empty, as it usually was this early on a Monday morning. Mia had been inside plenty of times to deliver eyewitness testimony or expert opinion on various cases, but she'd never sat at the table in front of the bench, in handcuffs. When the officer stood her in the back doorway to the room and told her to wait there, she gnashed her teeth so hard she almost heard them breaking.

"All rise," the bailiff said. "This court is now in session. The Honorable Michael Cressley presiding."

A pit formed in her stomach. Of course she'd get Cressley. Michael Cressley was a notorious hard-ass, and well-connected to the political world.

The courtroom was never like they showed on television. There was so little drama, so little in the way of shocking confessions and gavel banging; most of the time, it was enough to make most people yawn.

But as the judge came in, Mia had never been more alert.

The man with a head of full white hair, climbed to his bench, never looking at her until he'd pulled up his chair, then glanced at the folders and laptop in front of him.

When his eyes met hers, it was with more than a little contempt.

"The first matter we have to pick up is the case of the State of Texas against Mia North."

The two guards motioned her forward, to the podium. A young, blonde woman, who looked like she was fresh out of law school, was standing there, gnawing on a pen cap. *Her* lawyer? Mia had never seen her before. Was she friend or foe? Who'd hired her? "Who are you?" she whispered.

"Your attorney," the woman said in a prim manner. "Your father sent me. Let me handle everything."

Mia felt a pang of longing for her father. When he'd been over, earlier in the weekend, she'd taken him for granted. Barely talked to him. He'd sent her this message from afar, a lifeline, but her heart ached with the shock it must've been to her parents. He had a bad heart—this news probably didn't help.

She nodded.

"This is for the arraignment and indictment for Mia North for the events of twenty-one August of this year. Counselor, do you have a copy of the indictment?"

"Yes, your honor."

The judge nodded. "Mia North, you understand you are being tried for capital murder in the case of Ellis Morton Horvath?"

She nearly choked. Her knees wobbling so much, she had to place her clammy palms flat upon the table in front of her.

"Mia North?" he asked. "Do you understand that?"

The woman nodded at her, encouraging. Mia finally managed a nod.

"You should be aware that should you be found guilty, the sentence for a capital felony in Texas is either death or life in prison without the possibility of parole," the judge continued.

Death.

The word hung in the air, crowding out all others around it.

Mia had been through danger in her life, but right then, she'd never felt so impotent. She clasped her hands together—they were so slick with sweat it was a wonder she couldn't slip the handcuffs right off. *Calm down, Mia. You're not going to be sentenced to death. This is not going to happen. They're going to realize their mistake soon.*

"Mariam Walters, you've had a chance to review the indictment with your client, yes? And how to you choose to plead?"

"Not guilty," the other woman spoke.

Mia stared at her. Yes, that was what Mia had expected her to say, but did she review the charges? She barely even knew who this woman was. Had Pembroke arranged this for her?

"Plea of Not Guilty is entered," the judge said in monotone, glancing at the clerk "And the trial will begin . . . February first?"

The clerk said, "Yes . . . er, actually February second is the Monday."

"Okay. Any idea how long this trial will take?"

At first, she thought he was speaking to her, but then a man behind her, with a gruff voice, said, "With jury selection, ten days."

She glanced over her shoulder to see a man she'd seen often, however, never from this vantage point. It was Vince Cappela, the state prosecutor. Usually, he'd have a smile for her, a wave. Now, he seemed to look *through* her, as if she were nothing but air.

The woman next to her said, "As far as the matter of bail goes . . . we'd like to—"

"Bail's denied," the judge said, reading from a paper. "Prosecution is concerned with the defendant's in-depth knowledge of police procedure; she might represent a flight risk. Any additional motions?"

"No, your honor," the attorney said, defeated.

Too soon. She'd given up too soon. What would happen during the actual trial? Would Mariam Walters fight for her, then?

Mia stared, her knees now dangerously close to giving way. The trial was months from now. That meant that the earliest she could see Kelsey would be . . .

She swallowed the sob in her throat. Maybe never.

The reality of the situation crashed down as the judge's gavel came down hard, dismissing her. The attorney touched her shoulder and said, "We'll meet tomorrow to decide on a game plan," but that did little to soothe her. What game plan? Was there any point?

No matter what, Mia knew she would be going to prison for a long, long time.

CHAPTER SIX

"Next," a gruff voice said.

Mia stepped forward, feeling like she was in the midst of some terrible fever dream. Around her, the gray walls of the prison seemed to clench, growing ever-smaller, the farther she stepped inside.

The bus ride from the courthouse had been surreal. She'd looked out at the neighborhoods she'd considered to be her home for most of her life, wondering if she'd ever have freedom again. Even just the thought of walking through the thick grass of her lawn seemed impossible now. Breathing the air. Feeling something other than this massive weight, pressing down on her.

At the front of the line, a woman behind a wire mesh netting said, "Name?"

"Mia North," she said in a wobbly voice that wasn't her own.

The woman marked something on her computer and motioned with her chin. "Move aside for processing."

She was herded along into a locker room, where officers surrounded her. A guard mumbled, "You have any money, personal effects, jewelry . . .?"

She shook her head. "They took all of that already," she said softly, wondering if she'd ever get it back. She'd been wearing a faux pearl ring her daughter had given her for Christmas. It'd been plastic, and turned her finger green, but Kelsey had been so proud of it. It'd been the first gift her daughter had ever given her, and so Mia did due diligence to make sure she always had it on. Now it was gone.

They guided her into a tile bathroom area. "All right. Strip. Into the showers."

The water was tepid, bordering on cold. Her skin ached for a long, warm, steamy shower to wash all this unpleasantness away, but she was trundled through as if on a conveyor belt, barely having time to wash her hair.

It had gotten plenty wet, though, and she didn't have time to wring it out before they handed her plain white undergarments and an orange jumpsuit, and paper-thin socks. Dripping all over the clothes, she pulled them on, shivering as water dripped off the edge of her nose.

The prison was dungeon-cold; she shivered as they ushered her along, barking out orders behind her. Stay there. Move. Turn. Stop. Go.

They handed her sheets, a blanket, a flat pillow, and a small bag of toiletries—toothpaste, soap, a toothbrush and comb. A female guard led her out into the prison itself, and that's when she heard the taunts and jeers of the other inmates.

She knew the north tower of the Dallas County Jail was the general holding area for women for all kinds of violent crimes. As she climbed the metal steps, she mentally went through her roster of recently solved cases, wondering if she'd had a part in bringing any of these inmates to justice for their crimes.

If any of them would be waiting for her.

And not because they wanted to give her a welcome party.

Hands reached out from behind the bars, close to, but not quite touching her. People banging on the bars, the clanging of metal against metal grating her ears.

"*Pspspspspss* . . ." some of the women were taunting, sounding like they were trying to lure a cat in an alley. "*Here, kitty, kitty, kitty.*"

"Oh, yeah, that's a cute one. Look at Miss Prissy with her pretty curls," another low voice said. "She won't last a day in here."

Mia already knew they were talking about her. The shower had turned her hair into a frizzy mess, but her mother had always said her shiny chestnut waves, a far cry from the stick-straight platinum of her sister's, were the envy of every woman in town.

Raucous laughter erupted. Cheers. Mia thought the narrow catwalk leading to her cell would never come to an end.

But at the very last cell, the guard stopped and stood at an open door. She glared at Mia as if she was a subhuman species. Mia quickly stepped in and stood at the open door, looking at the bare gray walls, impossibly small, closed space without a window to speak of. She wasn't prone to claustrophobia . . . until now.

Behind her, the guard mumbled, "In."

As stifling as it already felt, she looked down and realized that most of her body was still outside the cell.

When she took the step that would put her completely inside, fresh dread washed over her.

There was a loud, scraping buzz above her, and the door slammed shut with such finality, it echoed in her ears.

"Lights out," a guard yelled, and only a second later, she was cast in darkness. Not full darkness, though—there were dim lights emanating from the center of the prison, casting the shadow of her prison bars over the ground at her feet.

She looked around the shadows, wondering how on earth she'd ever sleep here. The jail had been one thing. That had felt temporary. This? This seemed permanent.

On the bunk bed, two mattresses were rolled over an uninviting metal frame. Mia unrolled the bottom one. She set her neat square package of worn sheets on top of the thin mattress and sat on it, burying her face in her hands. At least she didn't have a cellmate, she thought, as the chatter in the cells gradually faded to absolute silence.

"Pspspspsps . . . here kitty, kitty, kitty."

At first, she thought she was imagining it. But then it came again. It sounded like it was coming from the cell, right beside her.

"You there? Hey. Mia North. Agent Mia North. . .," a voice whispered.

She strained in the darkness and saw thin fingers, with long nails, waving at her.

Mia stiffened.

"It's me. Angel Vasquez. Remember me?"

The name struck a chord inside her chest. Angel, who'd cried at her boyfriend's sentencing. He'd jacked a car with an innocent woman inside, threw her out on the street, putting her in a coma. A real fine, upstanding citizen.

The day the man was sentenced, Angel had stalked out in her stiletto heels, pointed a finger at Mia, and shouted, "You bitch! You gonna pay!"

"You put my baby daddy in prison," she snarled. "I had no choice but to do what I had to do to support my kids. And now I'm in here."

There was quiet. Mia closed her eyes.

You need to be tough, Mia. Even if you don't feel it, act it. Don't ever let them see you react. That's what they're looking for. The reaction.

Funny, it was something she'd told Kelsey, when she'd had issues with bullies in second grade. She never thought she'd be dealing with it herself.

But these bullies wouldn't just steal her lunch money. They'd draw blood.

Suddenly, the woman's laughter rang out, clear and edged with a bit of insanity. "But now, so are you. And you better watch your back. Because the next time I see you, I'm cutting you so deep they ain't even gonna be able to scrape the rest of your sad-ass body off the floor."

*

The night dragged on, and even Angel eventually stopped chiding Mia and went to sleep. Sounds were everywhere, though. People arguing. Coughing. Alarms. Sounds coming out of the guard's radios. Guards laughing in the hall, patrolling the floor, their footsteps echoing hollowly on the metal floor and concrete below.

Mia lay flat on her back, staring at the bunk over her. It felt like a year had passed, and yet she knew it had only been hours.

Life in prison. That's what you get for capital murder in Texas. If you're lucky.

No, only the worst of the worst got the death penalty these days, but it was still a possibility.

When her doors slid open, she thought it was morning. But she was wrong. It was still too dark, the lights outside her cell blazing.

The guard knocked on the side of the door and stepped aside. "Wake up, North. You got company."

Another prisoner sauntered in. She was large, so wide she had to turn sideways to fit through the opening, face, puffy and scarred, mouth a straight line. From her expression in the dim light, her familiar mannerisms, it was obvious this wasn't her first stint in a place like this.

So much for her one saving grace—not having a cellmate.

Once again, the doors slammed shut.

The woman grunted a little as she got her bed ready and climbed up, without a word. The springs creaked in protest as she settled in with an exaggerated sigh of relief, and soon began to snore contentedly.

For a moment, she imagined Angel getting all the other prisoners together, and having them gang up on her. If Angel made friends with her new cellmate, she might never be able to find refuge, *anywhere*.

This can't be real. This can't be real, she chanted in her mind.

38

But everything around her told her differently.

It told her she was screwed.

She rolled over to face the wall, covered her nose and mouth with her hand, and it was only then that she allowed herself the luxury of a tiny, muffled sob.

CHAPTER SEVEN

Sixty-four.

That was the number of springs on the underside of the bedframe. Mia had spent much of that first night, running her finger over the imprint of the missing ring on her pinky, and listening to the woman above her, snoring as if she was getting the best night of sleep of her life.

In the morning, noises and light grew. Mia rolled over on her side, watching the guards on the landing below. From her vantage point, she could just see the tops of their heads.

Breakfast will be next. Angel Vasquez and her cohorts will see me, and I'll be dead.

She winced at the sound of the alarm. That was her cue to get up and out of her cell. She rolled up to sitting, but to her surprise, when the door to her jail cell sprang open, a guard stepped inside.

"North. Up."

She stood, smoothing back her hair, and took a tentative step forward. "What is this for?"

The woman simply said, "Come with me."

Mia followed her outside. She stepped quickly past Angel's cell, hoping she was asleep. But almost at once, the "*Pspspsps . . .*" started.

Mia straightened, clenching her fists in dread.

"Good morning, kitty," she taunted as Mia reached the stairs and went down to the first floor. She could hear her taunts, even as she reached the bottom of the steps. The guard did nothing to stop her.

The guard motioned her toward a pay phone. "You've got one call."

She let out a gasp of relief and surprise and practically lunged at the phone. Picking up the receiver, she dialed the numbers carefully. Her one shot, she had to make sure she did it right.

"Hello?"

Her lower lip trembled at the sound of her husband's voice. "Aidan?" she said, voice cracking.

"Oh, my God. Mimi? Is that you?" His voice cracked to match.

Mimi. His nickname for her, ever since they'd met, almost eighteen years ago. *Screaming Mimi,* since at the time, she'd been in college, dancing on a bar, a little tipsy. She'd told him, the first time he used it, no one ever called her that. She'd let him be the first, and it stuck. His Screaming Mimi.

Now, though, it felt like she'd been beaten into silence.

Tears flooded her eyes, but she blinked them back. She needed to be level-headed for this call, not a blubbering mess. "Yes. It's me."

"Oh, my God. Mimi. We've been going insane trying to understand what's going on. What happened? Obviously it's all just some big mistake. I told the press that when they called. I spoke with your parents. He said he had a lawyer—"

"Yes, I know. She came to the arraignment."

"And what happened?"

"I'm being indicted for murder. And of course, I pled Not Guilty."

He let out a noise that sounded like a wail of despair. "This is insane. Insane. Why isn't your supervisor, that guy Pembroke, doing something about that? Speaking on your behalf?"

"He's doing what he can." She looked around nervously, just imagining what the press was saying about her, now. If the news was spreading that rapidly, she'd likely have to watch her back for more than just Angel. "I'm not really sure if there's a time limit for this call, so just listen to me."

"But it's a mis—"

"Aidan," she said cutting him off. She knew he had questions, and she had them, too. But she also knew that he'd be wasting his breath asking them, because she didn't know the answers. She twisted the cord in her hand. "Just let me talk, okay?"

"Yes. Sorry. Yes. Of course."

That was Aidan, always trying to provide solutions. He didn't feel useful unless he was offering his two cents on a subject. But this was way out of his league.

She took a deep breath. "Yes, of course it's a mistake. I got the call and went to Ellis Horvath's apartment, we fought, and I shot him. But they're thinking I did it on purpose, because I had some vendetta against him. Because of the past. You know."

"That's ridiculous," he said. "You wouldn't—"

"We all know that. But unfortunately, no one else seems to. So I'm here. Charged with capital murder. The lawyer tried to get me bail but

41

it was denied. I think I'll be meeting with her again today to see what can be done," she said. "That's all. I don't have answers to anything else. Not yet. I'm sorry."

"That's okay. Just . . . I'll keep calling Pembroke. The FBI should be able to get you out of there."

She didn't have the heart to tell him she'd tried that. Besides, she needed someone out there to be fighting for her. "Okay. Yeah. Thanks." She had a thousand other things to tell him, but all seemed to fall by the wayside, except one. "How's Kelsey?"

"She's well . . . she's missing her mom. Not a minute goes by that she doesn't ask about you. I told her there was a mistake, and we're working on bringing you home, but . . ."

Mia swallowed the lump in her throat. "Is she there? Can you put her on?"

"Yeah . . . one second."

A pause, and she could hear the sound of his footsteps, probably climbing the stairs to her bedroom. A moment later, "Mommy?"

Mia swallowed that second lump and forced brightness. "Hey baby girl! How is my big girl doing? I hope you're not giving your daddy too much trouble?"

"Fine, Mom, but I miss you. Where are you? Daddy says you went away? Why won't you come back?"

"Yes, yes. I did, I'm away, and I can't come back just yet. But I'm trying--"

"Billy Sheridan says you're in the slammer."

Mia closed her eyes and let out a defeated sigh. Damn those next-door neighbors of hers, the Sheridans. Their twelve-year old boy was entirely too provocative, and seemed to love saying things to get Kelsey riled. "Where did he hear that?"

"He heard it on the news. He said you were like, the top story? Is that true? Are you in jail, mom? Dad won't let me turn on the television."

She sighed. "Well, yes. But I didn't do anything wrong, Sweetie."

"He said you murdered someone."

Her lips twisted. "That's the story. But it's not true."

"That's what I told him, Mom. I said you could never do anything like that and that he needed to shut his big fat pie-hole."

"Right! Yes." She clenched her teeth. "Well, I don't like you saying things like that. But you are right. It's all just a big mistake.

42

They think I did something that I didn't do, so I have to go to court and tell them. And I'm working with a bunch of very smart people, my co-workers and friends, who are going to help me figure it all out. So there's nothing to worry about. All right?"

"Uh-huh. Okay, Mommy."

She cradled the receiver between her shoulder and her cheek and went to touch the indentation on her pinky finger. "Okay, love. Listen to me. I love you very much. Be good. Do your homework."

"But Mommy. I don't want you to—"

"I know. But you're Mommy's strong girl. And I need you to be good. For Daddy. And I promise, I'll see you soon."

A longer pause. Kelsey was crying. Her words, muffled, came out in a tumble: "I love you, too, Mommy."

"All right. Put your dad back on," she said quickly, before she could break down.

"Okay, Mommy."

She wiped a stray tear from her eyes and sniffled. A moment later, Aidan was back. "All right, well, when can I see you?"

She shook her head and let out a laugh of exasperation. "I don't know. Just—talk to the lawyer. Mariam. I'm sure she'll be the easiest way to get in touch with me right now until we figure things out."

"Time's up," someone barked behind her.

"I've got to go," she said. "Please, just—"

"I love you, Mimi. We'll figure this out. I promise you."

He was her big problem solver. That was what he lived for. He sometimes joked that it was what he'd been put on this earth to do. But right now, this problem seemed unsolvable.

"I love you, too. Goodbye," she said, and when she hung up, she felt as if she'd left part of her heart behind, and there was no way of going back to retrieve it.

*

Mia wasn't ushered back up to her cell right away. Instead, she was led down the hall, to a section of the prison she'd never been to. She could smell eggs and burnt toast and assumed she'd be pushed into the cafeteria for breakfast.

Not that she was hungry. The thought of her family, out there, without her, had settled nausea deep inside her. It was an anxious gnawing, eating away at her.

This would destroy Kelsey. Forget about her having a normal life, after this. And Aidan? He didn't handle stress well. He needed her.

They always say life can change on a dime. For good, for bad. And sometimes, there's no way of going back.

Instead of following the scent of breakfast, the guard led her into a small conference room.

Mariam Walters was there, notepad in front of her, waiting. Her hair was up in a clip with tendrils falling down over her eyes, and she wore glasses that were much too big for her petite face.

"Agent North," she said, standing and shaking her hand. "Can I call you Mia?"

Mia shrugged.

"Mia. I'm sorry we didn't have a chance to be properly introduced before. I'm Mariam Walters. Your father asked me to step in as your attorney."

Mia sat down. "Yes. How do you know each other?"

"My father was on the Dallas police force with your dad. Ferris Walters?"

She nodded, even though the name didn't ring a bell. Samuel Clopecki, her father, had been a lieutenant in their precinct. Over twenty-five years on the force, he'd amassed quite the legion of friends and admirers. "That's nice."

"Yes. First things first. I was able to get your trial moved up, in light of bail not being provided. Jury selection is currently underway, so we have it scheduled for October fourth."

"I have no other engagements," she muttered sulkily, then blinked. Wait . . . October fourth? That was soon. Two weeks. Was it possible that all of this could be over so soon? Just like that? "Does that mean they think that I'm innocent?"

"No . . ." the woman started to scoot her chair in. "It just means the trial was moved up, and I need your help to answer all my questions, as plainly as possible, so I can build the best defense."

Still feeling pangs of longing for her family, Mia leaned over the table in desperation. "I need to know what you're going to do to get me out of here."

44

Mariam frowned. "Mia. It's not that easy. These are very serious charges."

"You don't think I know that?" she snapped, annoyed. "But the fact is, I'm innocent."

She nodded. "I know. I know. But I've been looking into the evidence they're amassing against you, and it's quite convincing."

"Evidence? I shot him in self-defense."

"But you can understand what it looks like."

She leaned in even more. "No. I know that it should look like I'm innocent, because I am. But they're drawing other conclusions. I don't know why."

Mariam shook her head and shuffled some papers in front of her. She had a folder with Mia's name on the tab, and it was already at least an inch thick. "Horvath had been calling your house, time and again, pranking you, saying vile things about what he was going to do to your daughter. Yes?"

Mia nodded, the man's silky, sick voice ringing in her ears: *I'm going to pop your sweet girl's cherry. I think I'll like that very much . .*
.

"You reported it to the authorities more than once, and yet nothing was done. Yes?"

She shrugged. It was all true. "That's right. Three times."

"You also reported, once, a man lingering in the bushes outside your house. Correct?"

She nodded. Again, true. "The police came out, but by then, he was gone."

"And twice, you called to report seeing a gray Toyota Camry driving slowly past your daughter's bus stop."

"No," Mia said, wanting to be crystal clear so that nothing about this conversation, which was clearly being recorded—her attorney kept fiddling with something under the table—could be misconstrued. "I reported it the first time, when my daughter said a man drove by the stop real slow. But I wasn't there."

"You left your eight-year-old alone at a bus stop?"

"I'd had a meeting for work, but I hadn't thought anything of it because there were a lot of other children and parents there at the time," she said, a bit defensively. "After that, after she told me about it, I stayed at the stop. I saw the car stopped, about a block from our neighborhood. Someone was watching. But it peeled away when I tried to approach it."

Mariam nodded.

"And," Mia added, pointing to her pile of papers. "If you look into it, there's a gray Camry registered to Ellis Horvath. So."

She raised her hands to the sky, like, *Draw your own conclusions.*

Mariam flipped a piece of paper and nodded in agreement. "Okay. So it's clear this man was a thorn in your side, and had been, ever since . . ."

"Last August."

"So, for over a year?"

She nodded. "That was when he got out of prison. He was sentenced for two years, for child pornography, but had his sentence reduced to six months."

Her eyes flooded with sympathy. "And he's been on you for that long?"

Mia nodded. "He was not incessant, though. Sometimes he'd wait a month, two. We went the whole summer without hearing from him. And then I got that call . . ."

"The call Saturday afternoon?"

She nodded. "It was funny. I'd almost all but forgotten about him. When I answered the phone, it was from an unknown number, and I know I should've suspected, but I didn't even think it could be him. And then the voice was Sara's . . . and she gave me his address . . ."

Mariam wrote something down in the margin of the pad. "But he had been harassing you for quite some time. And there was a call from his number placed to your house. The authorities are saying there's no real sign of a struggle."

"He shot at me first. And—"

"But there's no evidence of that. The police said he didn't even have a weapon."

"That's impossible. If they're saying that, then someone is setting me—"

She held up a hand. "Here's what they're saying. They're saying that you'd become fed up with him, and decided to do something about it. So you went to his place and shot him in cold blood."

"That's bullshit." She shrugged. "Ask David, my partner. Did you? He'll tell you. I wasn't on edge or on some vendetta. I was responding to a call."

46

She nodded. "David Hunter was interviewed extensively after the fact. He said you'd told him to meet you there, but that you rushed in, by yourself, before he arrived."

"That's right."

"He spoke very highly of you, but he did also say you took a lot of these crimes against children to heart. And you were especially rattled by Ellis Horvath's stalking of you."

Mia let out a long sigh. *Great, David. Thanks a lot.* "Ms. Walters. Do you have children?" she asked, already suspecting, from the age of the attorney, the answer.

"No."

"He told me he was going to tie me up, and fuck my eight-year-old daughter while I watched. I think any parent would be rattled by that."

Mariam recoiled, visibly shocked. "Yeah. I see. I understand that." She tapped the legal pad with the tip of her pen. "And unfortunately, it gives you all the more reason to have done what they accuse you of."

"No," Mia said. "It gives me all the more reason to have rushed in, like David said. I've been successful in solving many previously closed cases because of my methods. And I had every reason to believe that Sara Waverly was in there, and that she was in trouble."

"But you were wrong."

"This time, maybe. I wasn't wrong with Chloe Braxton. My intuition is usually spot-on, though. I knew there was danger in there. I just didn't realize what the danger was. That I'd be walking into a trap."

She raised one blonde eyebrow. "You think Horvath was setting a trap for you?"

"No. But someone was. Someone who was trying to frame me."

Mariam closed the folder, and closed her eyes, as if Mia's words had given her a raging headache. "Mia . . . Who would do that?"

"I don't know. If I were out, I might be able to find out. But I'm a little tied up, in case you didn't notice. So I need *you* to—"

"Mia. That's not my job. My job is to make sure I advise you in the best way so that you get the shortest sentence possible. I—"

"*No* sentence," Mia spoke over her. "I should get no sentence. I didn't do it. That's the only outcome I'll accept."

The attorney looked down at her papers, speechless.

Something dawned on Mia. "What are you saying?"

"Well," she said, lacing her hands in front of her. "It's my job to advise you, and with the evidence they have against you . . . I think you should change your plea to guilty."

"What?" Mia slammed both open hands on the top of the table and looked around in disbelief. "That's not happening."

"Listen to me, listen to me," she said, her voice syrupy sweet. As Mia had suspected the first time she met her, too nice for the courtroom. This is what she got when her father decided to call in a favor. "If you plead guilty to murder, instead of capital murder, I can get you a reduced sentence, since your record on the force has been exemplary. You could be out of prison in five years, Mia. Five. You can be there for your children when—"

"No." Was that supposed to make her feel better? Five years, in a place like this . . . she couldn't survive it. "I'm not pleading guilty to something I didn't do. And that's final."

Mariam frowned. She closed up the folder and began to pack everything into her briefcase. "You have time to change your mind. If—"

"I won't."

Mariam closed the briefcase latches with a snap and stood up. "I'll do my best. But don't expect miracles."

Mia didn't expect them. But she knew she needed one.

CHAPTER EIGHT

It was lunchtime by the time Mia finally got her first taste of the cafeteria.

The smell, though, was oddly the same as breakfast—a pungent aroma of something burned or burning, mixed with a slightly stale stench of day-old garbage.

This time, when the alarms sounded, the doors to all the cells sprang open at once. Mia swung her legs over the side of the bed just as the larger, older cellmate did the same. She jumped from her place with remarkable grace for her size and gave Mia a stoic look, like, *Watch it.*

"Sorry," Mia said, letting her step out first, and mimicking her moves. She was so large that the orange jumpsuit stretched to its limit over her backside and the melons of her chest.

Mia quietly followed her as the women proceeded silently down the metal catwalk. She managed a glance into her neighbor, Angel's, cell, and saw that it was decorated almost as fully as Kelsey's bedroom at home—except she had crosses and paintings of Jesus, mingling with Playgirl centerfolds.

Mia shuddered. She'd be in the cafeteria, or if not, somewhere else. There were only about two-hundred inmates in the cell block. There was no avoiding anyone, here.

The cafeteria was not much different from the cafeteria at Quantico—except here, the servers were safely hidden behind wire mesh dividers. Mia obediently took her tray, following the example of those in front of her, and accepted the food from the server.

It was a dark, tomato-y beef-a-roni, along with a piece of white bread.

Kelsey would be thrilled, Mia thought as she grabbed a package of plastic utensils. *She always begged me for Chef Boyardee.*

Mia had never made it for her, though. She hadn't thought it'd be nutritious enough. Apparently, the city of Dallas didn't care too much about the nutrition of their inmates.

Head down, Mia turned, spotted an empty table in the corner, and made her way to it. She sat down at a bench and slumped over her food, taking a first bite. It wasn't terrible, probably since by then she hadn't eaten in almost thirty-six hours.

She bristled as she felt a form, hovering over her.

Angel.

She was just about to turn around when the form lumbered past her and slid into the seat across from her.

It was her cellmate.

She didn't make eye-contact; she simply opened her package of utensils and dug in. For a moment, she simply shoveled food into her mouth. Then, she patted her mouth with the napkin, almost demurely, and said, very quietly, "My name's Shilah Summerhill."

She'd expected a gruffer voice from her cellmate. She'd also expected that the woman, as comfortable as she'd seemed in the cell, was in and out of these places, and good friends with Angel Vasquez.

Mia studied the woman, trying to judge any ulterior motives. She was probably a few years older than Mia, though her face was pitted with acne scars. Still, she had pretty, almond-shaped eyes, and bow lips that belonged on a movie seductress.

"I'm Mia," she said, deciding that she was safe. "You came in late last night."

She nodded. "I came from the Indian reservation upstate. The bus broke down three times." She snorted and pinched her side. "Probably because they were carrying this wide load. Ha!"

Mia stared at her, wondering how she could find anything to joke about in a place like this.

"First night in the place for you, huh?" she asked, finishing up her meal.

Mia didn't answer. She'd been working hard to let people think she was an old pro at this. Working, and clearly . . . failing. Instead, she pointed to her food. "Want this? I'm not really hungry."

Shilah reached forward, slid the paper tray over until it touched her massive chest, and dug in. "Don't have to ask me twice. They're all about portion control here. Like I care about portion control."

She watched the woman shoveling the food into her mouth for a moment. She'd told herself she would keep to herself, that it was probably the safest way to survive in here. But curiosity got the best of her. "How did you know?" Mia asked.

The woman looked up.

She looked around to make sure no one was listening. But the chatter was loud, echoing through the vast space. Her voice was a whisper. "That it was my . . . first time."

"Oh, that. Other than that you're turning down this fine culinary masterpiece? I was downstairs, in the office, waiting for my phone call. I heard you on the phone with your kid."

Mia cringed. Then she'd probably seen her cry. So much for acting tough, steeling herself so that nothing and no one got to her. Everyone in the place probably knew she was scared to death—she might as well have tattooed *Victimize me!* on her forehead.

"Word around this place is, you're some kind of Fed?"

Of course. She knew they'd talked. Her eyes swept around the place. It was probably just her imagination, but she felt like they were watching her. She suddenly felt naked, vulnerable. She put her hands on the table and went to stand.

Shilah smiled. "Look. I don't care. When you're wearing this orange jumpsuit, don't matter if you're Beyoncé. You're the same as all of us. Right?"

Mia studied her, trying to decide if she was telling the truth. Maybe Angel had gotten to her, and she was just trying to make her vulnerable, so she'd be an easy target.

"You should tell a joke."

The unexpected advice came out of left field, stirring Mia from her suspicions. "What?"

"Your kid. A joke. You know. I always have one on hand. Just in case. My son Rocky's fifteen, but he was only eight the first time I went in. I guess you could say I didn't learn my lesson the first time. But he always likes a joke, so when I get on the phone with him, I make sure I have one ready. How old's your kid?"

"Oh. Eight," she said, settling back on the bench.

"Girl or boy?"

"Girl."

She whistled. "Tough age. Old enough to know what's going on, but still so young that they miss their momma," she said with a shake of the head. "Anyway, you gotta always have a joke on hand. Like this. What's a pirate's favorite letter?"

Mia stared, her mind blank. "Ummm . . ."

"You probably think it's the *Rrrrrr,* but it be the C," she said in her best pirate accent, giving Mia a wink.

51

Mia cracked a smile. "That's a good one."

"Yeah. I think it's always good to get them to focus on something light and fun. You know. When you're in a good mood, so are they, right? Take their minds off the fact that you ain't with 'em."

Mia nodded. "You're right. Thanks for the idea." She leaned forward, now genuinely curious. "Your son is with his father?"

She shook her head. "No. His father's long gone. Last time, it was drugs, but that was his fault. I cleaned up my act and kicked him to the curb. This time, I got caught passing bad checks at work. Rocky's with my sister." She sighed. "Miss the little bugger, though. But he don't need me so much anymore. He's at that age where he wants to do everything himself. Bet your girl misses you. What you in for?"

Mia stiffened at the question. She wasn't sure it was proper etiquette to come right out and ask it, but apparently, this woman didn't care. And apparently, she hadn't heard anything from Angel through the grapevine. So that was good. Not *everyone* knew what she'd done.

But Mia's crime wasn't just a couple of bad checks.

She hesitated, then said, quietly, "Murder."

The woman let out a loud, raucous laugh. "You kidding me?" She slapped the table. "It's always the quiet, unassuming ones. What happened?"

"Just a . . . I shot a man. That's all."

She looked like she wanted to ask more, but just then, the obnoxious alarm buzzed overhead again, and everyone began to line up to return to their cells.

Shilah stood up and said, "Remember. A joke. It always works."

Mia followed the rest of the group, glad to not have to rehash the events of the past few days. Though one joke didn't make everything all right, it had helped. She promised to come up with a few for Kelsey, the next time she spoke to her.

*

Before long, things fell into a routine. Mia spoke with Mariam a few times, but it was mostly Mariam, trying to convince Mia to change her mind and plead guilty to the lesser charge of murder. She spoke with Aidan a few times, when Kelsey was at school, to get the rest of her information about the case. The rest of it, she learned from the news

52

programs, sometimes playing in the recreation area, where they were allowed to congregate a few hours every day.

So far, the news was the same: The state was convinced she'd killed Ellis Horvath, and wanted to seek the maximum sentence.

Meaning, the death penalty.

Though Aidan had promised that he would continue to speak to her colleagues at the FBI and see what they could uncover, so far, there'd been nothing. No smoking gun. No evidence to claim that she'd been set up for this terrible thing.

After all, who could've done it?

There were plenty of options. Like Angel Vasquez's boyfriend, every person she'd helped put away was a potential suspect. After nine years on the force, she had dozens and dozens of names. A good number of them were still incarcerated, but that didn't matter. She'd made enemies.

One morning, the women on the second level were led down to the locker room for their showers, a luxury they got only every third day. At that point, they were able to wash up, change their jumpsuits, and get new bedding for their mattresses.

"Hut two three four . . ." Shilah muttered behind her as they walked downstairs, mocking the guards. "Keep it up, two, three four."

Mia had grown to like Shilah. She was quiet, most of the time, but whenever she spoke, it was some joke or sarcastic remark that lightened the dark mood Mia was normally in.

At the entrance to the shower room, they shed their clothes into the big laundry bin and went into the vast, tiled shower. As it had been for her first shower, there was little steam, because the water was tepid. Mia went to the faucet she preferred, in the corner of the shower area, out of the way of the gang members and other frequent offenders who dominated the place. Facing the wall, she squirted shampoo from the wall dispenser and lathered up her hair, as usual, trying to get through the process as quickly as possible.

When she turned, wiping the water out of her eyes, she noticed only a blur of dark skin and hair tearing for her, and the blade of a shiv, slicing down on her.

She snatched her hand forward, just in time to grab a wrist before the point of the blade sliced across her collarbone. Letting out a cry, she whipped around, shoving Angel Vasquez back.

Angel, curly hair matted against her face, let out a snarl before advancing again, the blade in front of her. "I told you I'd get you, bitch!"

People around took notice and started to crowd around jeering. Mia glanced at the doorway but didn't see Shilah or any guards as the girl dove forward again, shrieking in rage.

Mia jumped aside, narrowly missing getting stuck in the midsection as she slid along the slick tile, falling to her knees. She felt the presence behind her, and even though she couldn't see the shiv, she could sense the tension in the air, feel the woman behind her, readying to dig it into her ribs.

The moment Angel reached forward, fisting handfuls of Mia's hair to pull her upright, Mia pushed off the slick tile floor with her knees and shot backwards, thrusting her elbow back sharply so that it connected squarely with Angel's nose.

Angel let out a howl, dropped the shiv to the drain, and covered her nose with both hands. Blood coursed between her fingers, mingling with the water. "Ow! You bitch! You broke my nose! Ow!"

The cheers quickly dissolved as Angel's crew realized just what had happened. They started grabbing towels to come to her rescue.

The crowd dispersed without a word as the guards arrived on the scene. "What's going on here?" one said as they came in.

Staying close to the wall, Mia skirted around the chaos, slipped away, grabbed a towel, and wrapped it around herself as she collected her new clothes and bedding. Any triumph she'd felt at seeing her fallen attacker was short-lived. That crisis had been averted, but there were plenty of Angel Vasquezes in here. She knew there would be more trouble, and she'd been lucky, this time. There was no telling how long her luck would hold out.

CHAPTER NINE

The Monday of the trial was a rainy, gloomy one. Mia noticed that especially because it was the first time in days that she'd seen the sky, if only for the few hours that they brought her from the prison to the courtroom downtown.

As expected, during that ride, she realized how much her perception of everything had changed. Everything seemed bigger, wider, more beautiful. And all of it seemed like a luxury—even the thought of her weekly supermarket trip, which she'd once detested. Even the fresh air, which she'd taken for granted, seemed lovely. She even thought about catching rain on her tongue, she'd missed it so much.

But she knew the thing that had changed the most was right in her own home.

Kelsey. Aidan. As much as he'd tried to tell her they'd manage, she was an important cog in the machinery that kept their household running. She knew her absence was tearing them apart.

Stupid me, she thought, again and again. *It was because I was so gung-ho about my job that I'm here in the first place. If I hadn't taken that call, if I'd just ignored it and gone on with the barbecue, I'd be home, waking Kelsey up for school, right now . . .*

She'd woken up early and done her best to make herself look presentable for the trial, but she didn't have her make-up bag or a nice suit to wear to garner sympathy from the jury. No, she was wearing orange, a color that screamed, GUILTY. Mariam hadn't even suggested much for the trial, at all. It was as if, once Mia had rejected the idea of a plea deal, Mariam had just given up.

Though they would be deciding her fate, it wasn't the jury that mattered the most to her, right now.

She was going to see Aidan. Kelsey. Her parents. She didn't want to worry them any more than she already had. So she'd tried the best she could to look presentable, with what little she had.

Her heart was pounding as they led her down the long corridor to the courtroom. It was the same courtroom as before, but now, even before she reached the open door, she could tell from voices emanating from the room that the place was packed. The bailiff said, "Jury is entering the courtroom."

When they led her out, her wrists shackled in front of her, she felt every eye in the place on her, trying to figure her out. *Did she do it? Is she guilty?*

Trying her best to ignore it, she immediately sought out her family. She saw them, standing awkwardly and anxiously in the front row, all of them looking as though they hadn't had a lot of sleep in the past few weeks. Aidan looked as though he'd been crying. As she followed the guard, she looked to his side. No Kelsey.

She was led to the table, close enough that she could speak to her family from her seat. Her father reached over and touched her shoulder. She tried to smile back gratefully. She asked her husband, "Where's Kelsey?"

"She's at school. The show must go on, even now." He smiled crookedly.

She couldn't return it. "But what about . . .?"

"Francine's taking care of it," he said, but there was something he wasn't saying. She could read it in his eyes. *I don't want her to see you looking like this.*

He was right. As much as her heart ached for her daughter, she didn't want Kelsey seeing her like this, either.

"All rise," the bailiff announced.

Mia turned around just as the judge appeared. The Honorable Michael Cressley, once again, with his thick swath of silver hair and bifocals.

She stood up along with the rest of the courtroom as he approached the bench. As he did, she glanced at the jury, the men and women who held her fate in their hands. They all looked like reasonable people. Surely, they'd find some doubt in the story. After all, the burden of proof was on the prosecution. *Theirs* was the uphill climb. All Mariam Walters had to do was provide reasonable doubt.

But as Mia's eyes shifted to her attorney, her own doubt crept in.

It grew even more when it came time to give the opening statements.

Vince Capaldi stood up, and in his typical, grandiose way, strode back and forth across the courtroom, pointing an accusing finger again and again at Mia.

"Ladies and gentlemen of the jury," he said, owning the room, thriving on the attention. "On the surface, Mia North is indeed everything a good woman should be. Homecoming Queen. Dallas Debutante. Top in her class at Baylor. Married for a decade, with a loving husband and child. But not only that, she was born with the need to serve, to see justice done, and it was probably that desire that led her to put in her application with the FBI. And it worked for her—she has an impeccable record—nine years as an agent with the Federal Bureau of Investigation, and the awards and praise kept coming."

Vince raised a finger. "But little did people know that Mia was a woman with a problem. A traumatic incident in her past led her to want to seek revenge at all costs."

Mia stiffened. *Sam Jr.*

"Yes. When she was a child, her own brother was senselessly taken from her family and murdered. And so it turns out, when it came to those who perpetrated crimes against children, Mia North was ruthless. She would stop at nothing to see those she found guilty punished. And if the justice system failed . . . well then she believed that she had no other choice." He shook his head sadly, then strode over to the jurors, looking several of them in the eye, in turn. "What I intend to prove is that when Mia North didn't feel that the wheels of justice had turned to her satisfaction to convict Ellis Horvath for the crimes he had committed, she decided to take justice into her own hands and shoot him in cold blood."

The jurors watch, rapt. Not a single one of them moved, or even breathed. It was only when he thanked them and nodded at the judge that Mia had a momentary thought: *Maybe I should've taken that plea deal.*

She shook her head slightly, nauseated by the thought.

No. I'm not a liar. I've never lied—not once—during my career. And I'm not going to let anyone force me to do it now.

Judge Cressley looked at Mariam. "Counselor?"

Mariam stood and began to speak, her voice quieter and less assured. She went into Mia's career as an FBI agent, her exemplary record on the force, and spoke of her family. Then she laid out the facts of the case briefly, and what she intended to show, but her remarks seemed half-hearted. Mia kept looking at her, waiting for her to drop truth-bombs that had the jury nodding, just as Vince had done, but it never happened.

Do more, she found herself urging her attorney in her head. *You haven't done enough yet.*

When Mariam thanked the judge and sat down, the hole in Mia's gut became a chasm. "What happens now?" she whispered to Mariam.

"The prosecution is going to call its first witness," she responded shortly.

Well, obviously. All she had to do was watch any courtroom drama on television to know that much. But from this vantage point, it was different. She didn't just want to know the schedule of events. She wanted her lawyer to give her impressions on how the case was going. Reassurances.

But Mariam Walters had none to give.

That wasn't the first indication that she was in trouble, but it was the strongest one. Her own attorney was just going through the motions. Her own attorney didn't believe her.

Vince Capaldi stood. "The prosecution calls David Hunter."

Oof. Right for the jugular. Turning her own partner against her.

There was a faint rustling to her right. She need only crane her neck slightly to see David stand, adjust his suit jacket, and proceed toward the witness stand for swearing in.

He didn't glance at her. Not once. When he took the oath and sat down, it seemed as though he was deliberately avoiding gazing at her. She was right in his line of vision, and yet, he regarded her like a stranger.

Once he'd stated his name for the record, Capaldi said, "You've been an agent of the FBI for . . . how long?"

He shifted in his seat. "Three years."

"And in that time, how long have you known the defendant?"

"All three years, sir. She was my partner from the very beginning."

"So you'd say she was the one in charge of showing you the ropes."

He nodded. "That's correct."

"So in that time, you'd worked long hours on cases together, and you'd come to know her fairly well."

He chuckled a bit to himself. "We used to joke that only her husband knew her better."

"You saw each other outside of work as well?"

He nodded. "Yes, sir. I came to her house for a couple parties; we'd get together for a few beers after work, sometimes. She'd ask how my son was, and I'd asked after her family. We were friends."

58

Were. As in, over. So even her own partner, the man she'd taken under her wing, was turning against her.

"She's a good agent, sir. Her help made me a better agent, too. There's no one better at what she does. That's why the whole thing came as a big shock to me."

He ignored the comment. "Did you work on the case of Ellis Horvath with the defendant?"

The smile disappeared from his face. "Yes, sir. He was one of my first cases."

"And as an investigator, what did you learn about Ellis Horvath while conducting that investigation?"

He took a deep breath. "Horvath was a child predator. There was no doubt about it. He was addicted to child porn, as evidenced by tens of thousands of images found on his home computer."

"Let the record show that Ellis Horvath was sentenced to two years in prison, but received a truncated sentence of eighteen months, with time off for good behavior," Capaldi said, bringing up a formal document on the screen in the front of the room. Mia gazed at the picture of the creep, a balding, thirty-something man with glasses. He looked so normal, a quiet, mild-mannered science teacher, like anyone's neighbor.

Sam Junior's killer probably had, too. That was why he'd never been caught.

"That wasn't the last you heard of Horvath, though. Was it?"

"No, sir. We assisted the Dallas Police Department investigation in the case of the murder of that little girl. Ashley Lopez. It was Agent North's belief that Ellis Horvath was involved in it. A witness had seen him jogging near where the body was found, and he didn't really have an alibi for the time of death. Plus, he clearly liked little kids."

"And what were your findings on that?"

"We found absolutely nothing to tie Horvath to the Lopez case."

"And yet she maintained a belief that he was involved. Why was that?"

He shrugged. "I can't speculate."

"Did you hear her say anything when she heard that he was not going to be tried for the murder?"

He nodded.

"And what was her reaction?"

He shrugged. "Sir, it's normal for us to get invested in cases. We all do. We work on them for weeks, months, and sometimes—"

"Answer the question, please."

He raised his palms to the sky. "She was disappointed. She didn't believe it. Even when the case was closed, she insisted on following up, digging up leads, despite us being assigned to other cases. I got nervous Pembroke—our Agent in Charge—would wring our necks. But when North gets an idea in her head, she chases it down, like a bulldog. And she doesn't let anyone get in her away. I think she went a little unhinged, trying to find something. But there was nothing."

Speculation, Mia thought, glancing toward her attorney. *That's speculation.*

Mariam Walters was gazing at something on her laptop.

Vince Capaldi continued, unhindered. "Unhinged?"

He nodded, seeming a little embarrassed to have used such a strong word. "Well, not unhinged, exactly. But she was intense. Sometimes a little irreverent. She doesn't always go by the book, but it pays off for her."

"What exactly, did she do that gave you the impression that she was maybe going off the rails?"

"She wasn't going off the rails—"

"You did say she was intense. Chasing after things like a bulldog . . . and that you were nervous your Agent in Charge would be upset."

Now, he looked beaten. "Yes, sir."

"Okay. Let me rephrase the question. What gave you the impression that she was taking this case a bit too far?"

He let out a sigh. "She said Horvath was the scum of the earth and didn't deserve to breathe air."

"He didn't deserve to breathe air," Capaldi repeated, pointedly, to the jurors. "Did she ever mention why she felt that way?"

"Yeah. She said that she thought he was stalking her. She thought she saw him at her daughter's bus stop, and that he'd called her a few times. She mentioned she'd reported it, but that the police weren't doing enough."

"What did you think about that?"

"Speculation," Mia muttered, leaning into her attorney.

David shrugged. "Well, the police looked into it, and found nothing to substantiate her claims. So after a while, we all thought she was a little paranoid."

"Objection," Mariam said, just when Mia thought she might let everything the prosecutor said go unchallenged. "Speculation."

The judge nodded. "Jury will disregard the witness's last statement."

But it was out there. Now, the entire jury thought she was not only unhinged, but paranoid, too. Her own partner had said so. They wouldn't simply forget that information, just because the judge told them to.

"Tell me," Capaldi continued, lacing his hands behind his back and pacing. "Have you ever seen her get carried away by any other cases?"

He met Mia's eyes for only a moment, and for a second, she could see the guilt in his eyes. *I'm sorry,* he seemed to say. "Well . . . yeah. Really any case where kids are involved. She goes hard after it."

"For example . . ."

"Well, there's the case of Chloe Braxton, the girl who was kidnapped. She wouldn't let that one go either. She kept doggedly chasing Wilson Andrews. Yes, the girl was found in a house belonging to him, but half the neighborhood belongs to him. The police looked into it and found he had an alibi for the kidnapping, and because he leased it out to several people, he had no idea she was even there. But she didn't buy it."

"Did you tell her she needed to cool it?"

He nodded. "Yes, sir. I did, and everyone did. I know Pembroke told her, several times."

"So you were not the only one who noticed her behavior as a little off?"

"No, sir."

Mia gritted her teeth and whispered, "Ask about Wilson Andrews's connection to Chloe Braxton. Ask about all the evidence against Horvath that was trashed because Lopez's crime scene was tampered with. Or—"

Mariam held up a hand. "Not yet. Wait for cross-examination," she murmured, writing something on her legal pad.

Capaldi continued on, "So she felt very invested in these crimes . . ."

"Yeah. Like I said, especially ones against children."

"Did she ever tell you why?"

"She mentioned some kind of family tragedy. I didn't ask more than that. But I heard through the rumor mill that she had a brother who was killed as a child, so she took these things personally."

"Objection. Hearsay," Mariam mumbled.

"Your honor, we have previously recorded the case of Samuel Clopecki, age seven, who was kidnapped and found murdered two decades ago." He held up a school photograph of a little boy with a gap-toothed smile, one Mia had seen in her parents' home time and again. Behind her, Mia's mother let out a little gasp. "The defendant's brother. Kidnapped when he was just seven years old. His body was found six months later, in a wooded area, ten miles north of town. To this day, the case remains unsolved."

Mariam said, "The prosecutor is attempting to link my client's mental state to a case that happened years ago and has no bearing on this murder."

"Overruled," the judge said. "I think it lends context to the defendant's mental state at the time."

Mia jumped up. "Your honor, I have a perfect record! Not even a parking ticket! I've never done even one single thing out of line in all my time as an agent—"

Mariam yanked her hard by her elbow, causing her to fall backwards on her chair, hard. The judge banged his gavel. "Be silent! Counselor, please remind your client that in this court of law, she is not to speak. One more outburst like that and she'll be removed."

Breathing hard, Mia slumped forward. Her defense was a sinking ship, and as the captain, she had no way of ever escaping unharmed.

*

Mia knew.

Days later, it was like she was going to her own execution by firing squad. As the guards led her in, she looked at the frightened faces of her family members—her husband, mother, and father—and had the feeling they knew it, too.

After so many days of trying to smile, to be the strong one, she couldn't do it anymore.

She'd sat there for the better part of a week, listening to the evidence piled up against her. The defense's arguments had been half-hearted, uninspired. No matter what she tried to tell her attorney to say,

62

Mariam seemed intent on handling things her own way. Driving her into the ground.

The jury had deliberated for less than three hours. And now, as they were led into the stand, one by one, not a single one made eye contact with her.

That was the kiss of death.

The judge said, "Jury, have you reached a decision?"

The foreman nodded, "Yes, Your Honor, we have."

"All right. Will the defendant please rise?"

Mia rose to her feet, knees wobbling. She braced her hands on the table in front of her to stop herself from toppling.

"In the matter of The State of Texas vs. Mia North, the jury finds the defendant guilty of the charge of capital murder."

Capital murder. The worst crime possible in the State of Texas.

The only people who seemed shocked by the announcement were in the gallery, letting out a gasp of surprise. Mia only crumpled, the words echoing in her ears. Behind her, her mother sobbed quietly. Her father let out a pained groan. Aidan said, "No. This is wrong."

But it was over.

The trial, her life. All of it.

The judge banged his gavel and spoke directly to her as she wavered, then falling back to her chair. Beside her, Mariam clutched her arm, but her expressionless face seemed to say, *I told you this would happen.* Mia didn't hear any of the words, really, only snippets of what was going on around her. *Life imprisonment. First possibility of parole in thirty years.*

This wasn't happening.

For shooting in self-defense a man she was sure had murdered an innocent girl, she was receiving punishment. She was going to be incarcerated in the state prison for life. The next time she'd be eligible for parole, her daughter would be the same age she was, now.

A single tear slid down her face. This time, she didn't even bother to wipe it away.

The judge banged his gavel, and people jumped up to leave. She expected she would have time to say goodbye to the people she loved, but in the next second, the guards had grabbed her, pulling her away. She took one glance at her parents.

Their lives had been destroyed. Again.

Aidan, his face full of horror and utter desperation, called, "Wait! Mimi! I--"

Across the courtroom, she saw him reaching out for her, waving something at her. Something that looked like the teddy bear that used to sit in a special spot on Kelsey's pillow at home. Kelsey had probably given it to him, to give to her mother, to keep her company. It was one of her favorites, but Kelsey was like that, always sacrificing for the good of others. It probably smelled like her No More Tears shampoo.

At that moment, Mia had never wanted anything so much.

But the door slammed behind her, and that was all. Maybe he was going to say he loved her, something she desperately needed to hear. But she felt too guilty. She'd destroyed his life, the life of her daughter, too.

She'd gone into the FBI to help people, to somehow avenge the death of her little brother. But not like this. Not by doing what they'd said she'd done. So many lives had been ruined. And it was all on her.

Never had she felt so terrible.

CHAPTER TEN

Back in her cell, Mia stayed in her bed, even after the alarm rang, signaling dinner. Tears fell freely, over her cheeks, soaking the thin mattress. She didn't bother to hide them, now.

What did any of it matter? Her life was over.

The doors slid open. Shilah, who'd respectfully stayed quiet after she'd returned from the courtroom, whispered, "You'd better come to dinner."

Mia ignored her. As far as she was concerned, she never wanted to eat, never wanted to do anything for herself, again.

"Come on," Shilah gently coaxed. "You're going to get in trouble if you stay here."

Mia rolled over and faced the wall. They could shove their gun between her shoulder blades and pull the trigger, for all she cared.

Moments later, she heard voices screaming her last name outside. "North! Don't make us come up there."

She ignored it.

Moments later, a guard marched in, standing in front of her. "Up, North."

"No," she mumbled.

The guard yanked her back. *"Now.* We're holding the rest back from dinner until you come eat. And I promise you, you think you're not popular now? Just wait."

She didn't care anymore about the wrath of the other inmates. Let it come on her. But she didn't want to keep people like Shilah, who lived for mealtime, from eating.

It took every bit of strength she had left to roll to a standing position and join the line.

She barely noticed the other inmates like Angel and her cronies whispering about her, the pungent stench of the meatloaf dinner, the fight that broke out in the lunch line ahead of her. Someone had fashioned a spoon into a weapon, and there was blood everywhere. Mia simply stepped over the mess, collected her foul meal and sat in her usual spot, staring at the rice on her tray until it blurred in front of her into one white mass.

"I take it, it didn't go well."

She didn't look up at the sound of Shilah's voice. She simply shoved her tray over to her. Shilah gladly accepted it, turning it over and adding it to her own plate.

As she scooped up her first forkful of meatloaf and runny mashed potatoes, she said, "At least you didn't get the death penalty, right?"

Though there was nothing in front of her, now, she stared at the table. "I'd rather be dead."

"Don't say that. You know what that little girl of yours would say, if given the choice between you being dead or in prison?" she asked, chewing heartily. "She'd want a living momma. There are worse things than being in here, I tell you. She'll visit you. You'll see."

"Thirty years. I won't see her for thirty years, at the least."

"You'll see her. She'll visit you every chance she gets, I'm sure."

Mia shook her head. "They're sending me to the Southwest Women's Correctional Center."

"Where's that?"

"New Mexico."

She'd had the same question. Her attorney had looked it up for her. The Southwest Women's Correctional Facility for Women outside of the desert town of Grants, NM, was over seven-hundred miles away, in the middle of the Chihuahuan Desert, a couple hours south of Santa Fe. It was the closest federal prison with room for a violent female criminal like herself.

She couldn't imagine being that far away from everyone she loved. That was the reason she never left Texas for school, why she was miserable her entire six months at Quantico. When she'd been given her assignment back home, she'd been so proud. She'd told Aidan she never wanted to leave Texas again.

And now . . . she was going. Alone. Even if they wanted to visit her every chance they got, those seven-hundred miles were going to make it awfully hard.

"You said your attorney wasn't up to the challenge," Shilah said, clearly trying to be helpful. "Maybe you get a new lawyer. What are your chances of appeal?"

Mia didn't know. She couldn't think of that, now. Yes, she'd need new representation. But did it even matter? She'd need new evidence, some reason for the appeal to be granted. And she didn't have that. Didn't even know the first place to look.

Besides, did she really want to go back to trial again? Her first trial had been so fast, and yet she was already tired of fighting. What was the point, when it seemed everyone was against her?

She shrugged and buried her face in her hands.

"Look," Shilah said. "Everything will work itself out. You'll see. New Mexico ain't at the other end of the world. You'll have visitations, and I'm sure your family'll be there. That little girl of yours. And—"

She stopped suddenly and glanced in the aisle. Mia could hear their shoes squeaking as they approached. "North. Get up," a guard said, standing in front of her. "You have a visitor."

A visitor. *Kelsey.*

Her heart jumped at the thought.

"That's strange . . .," Shilah murmured. "A visitor?"

Mia jumped up. So her father had decided to bring Kelsey to see her, anyway. As much as she didn't want her daughter seeing her like this, she needed to see her, to give her strength to get through the next few weeks. Or maybe it was just Aidan.

Whoever. Any friendly face would do. She found herself tripping over her own feet as she followed the guards. Once, she accidentally stepped on the guard's heel.

"Sorry . . . is it my husband?" she asked, the hallway seeming to stretch on forever. She tripped over her words just as much as her own feet. "My daughter?"

The guard simply shrugged and seemed to walk even more slowly. It was only when they had nearly reached the door for the visitation room that it suddenly struck Mia why Shilah had thought it was strange.

Visitation day was on Saturday.

Family was strictly not allowed until two to five, Saturday afternoon.

Her heard plummeted. That meant it was probably someone with clearance. Mariam, likely, here to tell her that it was Mia's own fault she'd gotten this horrible sentence.

Great. She stopped at the door. "You know what? I actually don't want to talk to her. You can tell her I'll be seeking other counsel for the appeal. Because there will be—"

"In," the guard barked, opening up the door and nudging her forward.

She stumbled in, only stopping herself from falling face first onto the ground at the last second.

When she looked up, her blood immediately froze in her veins.

Yes, it was someone with clearance, someone important, but it was not her attorney.

It was the man who was number one with a bullet to state senate. The honorable, revered Wilson Andrews.

He was sitting at the table, across from her, separated from the Plexiglass divider.

Smiling complacently, his fingers laced together, his suit clean and pressed. He looked like he was about to deliver a speech to his constituents, as if he'd spent all morning being primped and preened by his handlers on the campaign trail.

It was so fake, she wanted to gag.

He's lucky that divider is there, she thought, *or I'd lunge across and slap that smile from his face.*

Probably not the best kind of behavior, considering she was hoping to appeal her sentence for murdering a possible child predator.

He motioned to the chair, but she stood there, not daring to move a step closer. She was convinced Ellis Horvath was the devil, but this man wasn't any better. She was one-hundred-percent sure he knew what had happened to Sara Waverly.

"What are you doing here?" she sneered.

Still smiling, he reached over and picked up the phone receiver, then shrugged and mouthed, *I can't hear you.*

She didn't *want* to hear him. Not at all. Not a single word that came from his lying mouth. And she certainly didn't want to move closer to him. But the door behind her was closed. It seemed she had no choice.

She took three steps closer, still refusing to sit, and lifted the black receiver from its cradle. "Andrews, why are you here?"

"Oh, couldn't I come and pay my favorite FBI agent a little visit? Give you a *better luck next time* pat on the back?" His grin widened. "You are someone I'll be representing as State Senator, after all, even if you are, technically, a criminal."

It suddenly struck her. As a criminal, she wouldn't be able to vote. And even if she was, she'd never place her vote for this man.

She shook her head and eyed the cradle, ready to put the phone back on it. "Go away, Andrews."

He chuckled. "I just think it's amusing. Here I am, out on this side of the glass, despite all your efforts. And you're doing . . . what is it? A life sentence for capital murder? Well, that's the show. I mean, pretty ironic, considering."

She stared at him, trying to keep her expression even and emotionless.

"And I wanted you to know," he continued when it was clear she wasn't going to offer him a response, "I plan to be a much better pen pal with you than you planned to be with me. That's for sure. Now, tell the truth. You weren't going to write me when you put me in there, were you?"

Her scowl deepened.

"Were you?" he repeated.

She tilted her head. "The only thing I'd be writing to you is to ask what the hell you did with Sara Waverly."

His smile faded. "For the last time. I did not kidnap Sara."

She snorted. "Yeah, right."

He banged a fist on the table in front of him. "It's that attitude that got you in there, North."

"It doesn't matter where I am. I know where you belong. And that's behind bars."

He chuckled. "Too bad you can't do anything about that."

"You came here to tell me that?"

"No, I have so much to tell you," he said with a smile, pointing to the chair. "Won't you sit and make yourself comfortable?"

"Not a chance," she answered at once. She lifted up the receiver and started to place it back.

"Wait, wait, wait," he said, to which she stopped. "I think I have something of great importance to discuss with you. Something you're really going to want to hear."

"Unless it's the location of Sara Waverly, I doubt you have anything of interest to give me."

"Not even the unfinished business we had?"

She froze. *Unfinished business.* She met his gaze, full of hidden meaning, and her gut turned. "What do you mean?"

"Well, there's the matter of that little bird. The one you went through great lengths to find. Mia North, you're a hero. Don't forget that. Even if you are a murderer, too." He grinned. "She's doing better. They moved her out of the hospital. She still has some amnesia, and she's not talking, due to the trauma, poor thing. But the doctors and therapists think she'll make a full recovery. They think she might be singing soon. And that'll be a shame."

Little bird . . . *Chloe.*

"You'd better stay away from her," she warned.

He laughed. "You know my approval rating is sinking, thanks to your meddling. This little dust-up, even if it was proven false, has made me a little unpopular, and I can't have that," he said, shaking his head. "But there's still one thing I can do that you can't. My family is very powerful. I can help anyone I want to get away with murder."

She tightened her grip on the phone, gnashing her teeth.

"Or I can even . . . set someone up for one." He winked.

Her mouth opened. What was he saying?

"Andrews . . ." she warned. "If you even touch Chloe—"

He hung the phone up with great finality, still staring into her eyes with a sadistic smile. Then he waved his fingers at her, leaving her staring after him, cold. She clenched her hands into fists and watched him, shouting his name, knowing he couldn't hear a word of it as he escaped into the free world.

He had all the power on earth, all the resources at his disposal to stop little Chloe . . .

And here, he knew that Mia was absolutely powerless.

*

By the time she reached her jail cell, Mia was practically begging the stoic guard who'd escorted her.

"Look. I need you to get me in touch with Special Agent in Charge Matthew Pembroke, of the FBI DFW Field office," Mia said, not for the first time, as she gripped the metal bars of her jail cell.

The guard who'd just placed her behind those bars rolled her eyes. "Honey," she said, tossing her ponytail. "You need to stop thinking you're some big-time FBI agent anymore. These days, you are nothing but a murderer."

"He don't want to talk to your skinny ass, so sit it down," Angel chuckled from the neighboring cell. Ever since she'd had her nose broken, she and her cronies had laid her hands off Mia, but that didn't stop her from putting in verbal digs, whenever she could.

"No, you don't get it. A girl's in trouble. She's in a lot of trouble. I think Wilson Andrews is going to kill her if I don't—"

The guard laughed, clutching her thick, jiggling side, right above her sidearm. "Uh, sweetie. If you're going to lie, you'd at least better try a better one that that. Wilson Andrews, from the Andrews clan? The guy who's running for office?"

"Yes." She gnashed her teeth. "Just call Pembroke. Or let me speak to David Hunter of the—"

"Right. Sit down and shut your mouth. I don't want to hear another peep out of you. You know the rules. No calls."

Of course, no one believed her. Some bad publicity had gotten through, but the media still portrayed the senate hopeful as if he were the Second Coming. They always showed pictures of him, hanging around with Average Joes, working soup kitchens, delivering humanitarian aid over the Mexican border. He was a regular saint, in a lot of people's eyes.

Shilah was lying on her back, staring up at the ceiling. As the guard strolled away, she rolled over onto her side and propped her chin on her pillow. "You really think Wilson Andrews is going to kill someone?" she asked, doubtful.

Mia nodded.

"But he's a pretty important guy. Half the state of Texas loves the man. You know that, right?"

"Yes, I do. But underneath that million-dollar smiled is a very sick man. He kidnapped Chloe Braxton, and I think he killed Sara Waverly, too. Only no one will believe me."

Her eyes widened. "How do you know this?"

"Because *he* was my visitor. He told me." She shuddered at the memory.

"He *told* you?"

"Well, not exactly. But he insinuated that something's going to happen to Chloe. And now there's nothing—"

"Wait. Why would he come to you? Why would he bother?"

"Because he knows there's nothing I can do, in here."

"But why *you*?"

"I was the one who tried to get him put away. He basically came to gloat and tell me that there's nothing more I can do anymore. I was the only one who put a wrench in his plans. Now that I'm in here, he's completely untouchable." She clenched her teeth and began to pace the small area. "And . . . and I think he framed me for the murder of Ellis Horvath."

"He did?"

She shivered as she thought about it. But Andrews knew just what would get her out of the house—a child in danger. Especially if it were Sara Waverly. And everyone knew about how she felt about Ellis Horvath. So it only made sense that he'd done something to set her up, to put her out of commission for good. "Yeah. It makes sense. He wanted to get me out of the way."

Her mouth opened. "Wow. So . . . you really didn't do it?"

"No. I killed Horvath. But in self-defense. The police don't think so, but he was armed and I was in danger. I didn't go there to murder him out of some vengeance plan, like they said."

She gaped, stunned. "Wow. I believe you, but . . ."

Behind the cinderblock wall, Angel said, "I'm innocent too! *Please*, bitch. You're going to rot in here. Boo hoo."

"Actually, she's going to New Mexico tomorrow!" Shilah called back, then rolled her eyes. "I'm going to miss you, *chica*. But I'll be out in another few weeks, anyhow. At least, I hope. Got to get back to my Rocky."

Mia managed a small smile. "Well, at least one of us will be free."

Shilah gnawed on her lip. "I could—I don't know. Go to the police. Pretend I got a tip. Or something?"

She shook her head. From what Wilson Andrews had said, in a few weeks it would be too late. Chloe needed help, *now*. "I don't think I have that kind of time."

Shilah sighed, "This sucks."

It did, indeed.

Soon, it'd be lights out. Mia was wound like a clock, though. Ordinarily, there'd be no hope of sleeping, knowing that bright and early in the morning, she'd be headed to a new, bigger prison, seven-hundred miles from home. But now, she was even more wired. *Think, think, think* . . . she commanded her brain, but of course, nothing came.

She continued pacing until a face appeared at the door of her cell. It was the same guard, fiddling with the lock to open it. Mia rushed up to her, hopeful.

"I spoke with the warden. One call," the guard groused softly, yanking open the door. "Come on. Keep it quiet, all right? Don't want everyone else knowing. And you need to be done by lights out, so make it snappy."

"Yes, thanks," she said, though she had no idea what time it was or how much time she'd be allowed.

"Yo! I want a call, too!" Angel shouted. "That ain't fair!"

The guard lifted her bully stick and rattled it against the bars of Angel's cell. "Shut your hole and get back."

Sure enough, the whole cell block came alive, people screaming that they wanted their calls, too. They'd have more of a reason to hate her, now. But it didn't matter; tomorrow, she'd be gone. As the guard led her downstairs to the phone, she made her plans. Special Agent in Charge Matthew Pembroke was too important. He was likely in a meeting and wouldn't answer.

Even though he'd testified against her, she hated to admit that her best bet was David—the man was as tied to his phone as she had once been tied to hers. After all, though he'd provided damning testimony, he hadn't said anything that he didn't believe to be true. He was the most honest of agents out there.

She wouldn't be able to call him at the office. They probably had a rule that he couldn't communicate with her. Luckily, she knew his cell phone number by heart. One minute, two at the most. All she needed to do was tell him to put a guard on Chloe. That was the most pressing thing, for now. To keep her safe. She'd explain the rest later, if need be.

When she got to the phone, she dialed with trembling fingers.

One ring, two.

After the third ring, there was a click. Then: "This is David Hunter. I'm not available to take your call . . ."

No!

At the beep, she said, in a tumble, "David, it's me. Mia. I know you're probably not supposed to talk to me anymore, but I have no one else to tell about this who's capable of doing something to help. Listen to me. Chloe Braxton is in danger. I need you to have a watch put on her. Please. I'll . . ." she looked at the guard, who was watching her in doubt, shaking her head slightly. *The paranoid girl, still trying to create trouble.* "I'll tell you more if I can, later. Please. Do this for me."

When she hung up, she felt a rush of impotence. He wouldn't be able to do that. He'd only been an agent in the force for less than three years. He'd need a good reason for requesting that kind of manpower. And what would he tell them? His criminal former partner, the one in prison for murder, has a hunch?

This was hopeless. She needed to make other plans.

"Come on, lights out in five minutes," the guard said, grabbing her arm. "You need your rest. You have a big day ahead of you. You're on your way to New Mexico tomorrow."

Right. Seven-hundred miles away from Chloe Braxton, and the danger that waited for her. Chloe, who was probably going to die, alone, scared, and at the hands of a child predator. If only there was some way to let her know!

She swallowed. Tomorrow, during the transport to her new prison, she'd experience the closest thing to freedom that she would see for possibly the next thirty years.

That meant, the closest thing to . . . escape. The closest she'd ever be to being able to help Chloe on her own.

Was that even possible? Could she even do something like that?

As she settled into her mattress, the wheels in her head began to turn.

CHAPTER ELEVEN

True to their plan, directly after breakfast, a corrections officer corralled Mia as they waited to file into their cells and told her she had thirty minutes to prepare herself for the trip to the new prison, her home for the next thirty years or more.

Good.

She'd spent all night awake, staring at those sixty-four springs above her, planning. She couldn't count on David's help. She needed to do something on her own. If she could somehow get out, she could do this. Hightail her way back to Dallas and find Chloe and intercept Wilson Andrews before he carried out his plan.

But what she needed to think about first was . . . getting out.

Somehow.

She didn't have much to prepare. All she had to pack was a photograph of her family, taken last Christmas, a bible they let every inmate have, and her bag of toiletries. Five minutes, a hug and some good wishes for Shilah, and she was ready.

"Good luck!" Shilah called after her as she was escorted out. Angel Vasquez hissed at her and spit on her shoe.

They led her to an office, where they sat her down on a hard metal chair as they performed various processing duties that seemed to take most of the rest of the morning. She watched the officers intently, listening, gleaning bits of information.

Seven-hundred and twelve miles. One stop at Amarillo for fueling and lunch. Approximate arrival, nine PM. Single prisoner transfer.

Escape.

Would it be possible? If so, when? How? What would she do?

The guards shackled both her wrists and her ankles, limiting her movement. Then, they flanked her as they led her outside to the fenced parking lot, where her transport waited.

The shackles were really her only deterrent. Everything else seemed to work in her favor.

It was a small van, not any bigger than the Dodge Caravan Aidan had insisted they buy when they became parents for the first time. He'd thought all card-carrying good parents drove them.

As they settled her into the seat, behind a metal grated divider, separating her from the driver, she heard Aidan's voice. "We need a minivan. All parents drive minivans. It's important. For transporting kids' stuff. Right?"

She hadn't argued with him. They'd gone out and bought one, only to learn, not long after, that he hated driving it. Not only did it make him feel middle-aged, but it had no pick-up whatsoever. They'd traded it in, three months later, for a Jeep Grand Cherokee.

She found herself smiling wistfully as she flashed forward to the present. It smelled like salami, a stench that made her stomach roil, and it was unbearably hot and stuffy in the cabin, even with the door still open.

The overweight guard, who must've been from the new prison, finished joking with the female guard from the Dallas prison. He lumbered over to her, his round Santa-belly jiggling. One of the buttons, near the underside of his belly and likely out of his view, was popped open, revealing his straining undershirt. There were sweat stains at the armpits of the powder blue shirt.

As he leaned forward, breathing heavily, she caught sight of the nameplate on his pocket. C. Barker. He arranged the shackles so that not only were her ankles and wrists bound together, but she was tethered to the seat itself.

This was going to be a problem.

The guard nudged her into the seat, fastened the locks and pulled on it. Then he smiled, baring one missing tooth, and exhaled right into her face. His breath was hot and smelled like the lunchmeat mixed with stale coffee. "Comfy?"

"No," she complained, swallowing back her nausea. "It's so tight. It hurts."

"Yeah, well," he said, looking down at the shackles. "No one ever said being a prisoner was supposed to be fun."

"Yeah, but . . . I have to be like this for how long? Ten hours?"

The guard nodded. "Give or take."

She let out a moan. "Hey. If I have to stay like this for ten hours, I'm going to complain. The whole time," she whined.

He rolled his eyes and went to slam the door on her. Then he thought better of it, and loosened the shackles on her wrists. "Better?"

She nodded. *This, I can work with.*

"Good. We're not stopping until Amarillo. Even if you have to pee, doesn't matter. You can piss yourself. I don't want to hear a goddamn peep out of you. Not once. All right?" he said, sliding the door closed before she could answer.

It was only then that she noticed that not only had he not put the restraint through the loop between her legs that was supposed to tether her to the seat . . . he'd left the keys there, on the side of the seat.

Way to make this really easy, fellow. Almost *too* easy.

He went around the other side of the van, opened the door, and hefted his body into the seat. Slamming the door, he rattled the cage between them and the front seat. "On our way, Alice."

The guard driving the bus, who was busy drinking a bottle of Gatorade, capped it and looked into the back seat. "All right, Carl."

She started the engine and the van lumbered forward. Mia watched from her window as the bus stopped at a guard's station, then was waved through, onto the main roadway, leaving her former home-away-from-home behind.

The only air was from a couple of cracked windows in front. At first, it was merely uncomfortable, but as time wore on, it became unbearable. Because of the shackles, she couldn't even fan her face or shift very far in her seat. Sweat trickled down her temple. "Air conditioning?"

"Sorry, sweetheart. Air's broken," Alice said, turning on the radio. Alan Jackson crooned "Chattahoochee."

They'd barely made it out of the Dallas city proper when Carl reached for the crumpled paper bag between them and pulled out a second half of a salami hoagie. He pulled back the wax paper around it and took a bite, dribbling tomatoes and lettuce and oil down his chin.

The stench hit her in mere seconds. "I'm going to be sick," she mumbled, looking out the window. A sign said, *Amarillo 300 mi.*

He laughed. "Should've eaten more at breakfast, darlin'."

"If I had, you'd be wearing it right now," she said, side-eyeing him.

There wasn't anything more important to him than that sandwich, clearly, so she didn't think he'd stop eating, just because she told him. She also didn't think he noticed that his sidearm was right *there*, within grabbing distance.

If only she could get free, she could grab it in a second. She eyed the keys by her thighs. If she moved her wrists to the side, she could easily grab them.

When Carl reached into his bag to pull out a giant red Gatorade, she took the chance to move, grasping the keys before he lifted his head from his bag.

The bus lumbered on. Carl finished his sandwich but began burping, releasing horrible smells into the air every few minutes. He pulled out a copy of *People* magazine and started reading it, hooting about various different stories. Every so often, he'd guffaw and smack the metal grate.

"Woo wee, Alice, listen to this one," he'd say, holding up the magazine, as Mia quietly found the right key and stuck it into the lock. "There's a guy in Ogden, Utah, who holds the record for the most times he's found money on the street. You wanna know how much he's found?"

"I don't know, Carl," she said, disinterested.

Mia turned the key, very slowly.

"Over five-*thousand* dollars," he said with a shake of his head. "He's found money over three-hundred times. Most he ever found was six-hundred. At once. Can you believe that? Son of a bitch is a lucky guy. I only found a quarter, once."

"No, Carl," she muttered, not taking her eyes off the road, which had given way from buildings and homes to desolate, gently rolling hills, dotted with creosote bushes.

Mia had to admit, she actually kind of liked Alice. But she had other things to attend to. And Carl might have noticed those things, had he taken his nose out of the magazine. With every bump in the barren desert road, though, he seemed to look out the window, instead of at her.

Had he looked her way, he might have seen her, slowly but successfully loosening the shackles on her wrist.

The Zac Brown Band's "Chicken Fried" came on, and Carl began to bop around, singing along. Another bump, and she gave another yank. She felt the cuff around her wrist slacken, and managed to pull her hand out. The second one was even easier, probably because of her sweat-slickened skin.

She wiggled her hand back and forth a few more times, and was free. Keeping her hands in her lap, she waited for the right time, as they sailed past a one-streetlight town that was nothing more than a few ramshackle homes and a gas station.

On the outskirts of the town, she made her move.

"Hey," he began, holding up the magazine. "Listen to this, Alice—"

She dropped the cuff and dove for him, grabbing his gun. He let out a guttural oof. Before she could aim the gun, he grabbed her wrist. She reeled back, elbowing him in the chin.

"Aggggh!" he shouted, wrapping his other fleshy hand around the butt of the gun in his struggle to get back his weapon.

"Carl! No Carl!" Alice was screaming from the front seat.

She must've taken her eyes off the road to see the commotion, because suddenly there was the screech of tires. The van fishtailed wildly. Mia managed a glance out the front window, where she saw dust rising all round, the van careening for the bank at the side of the road as Alice spun the wheel wildly, trying to correct.

Then they were weightless for a moment, before everything was tilted on its side. Tethered to the restraints, her body had nowhere to go. Still fisting the gun, she braced for impact as Carl wailed in her ear, "Oh god oh god oh god . . ."

The force of the final impact was incredible, the sound ear-shattering, the pain exquisite as the van slammed down, on its side, upending itself. Glass shattered, raining down upon them, and dirt was shoveled into the space.

Carl's body fell on her, his shoe randomly connecting with her jaw, his fingers threading through her hair.

Then the van was skidding, down an incline, the rattling and sickening sound of metal twisting and breaking scraping through her ears.

Dust billowed up, catching in her throat and eyes, as the vehicle juddered to a stop.

Tangled with Carl's dead weight, she pulled his heavy limbs off her and felt for a pulse. She found it, thudding lightly at his throat. Then she reached down and pulled his keys from the place where they'd fallen, and ran her hand along the chain. She found the lock at her ankles, blindingly poking the key into the hole again and again before she was able to free herself.

She slid the gun into the waistband of her jumpsuit. Above her, the side window had shattered. Testing her muscles, making sure that there were no injuries, she squirmed her way out of the tangled remains of

79

the car, careful to avoid the jagged edges of glass. She hefted herself out of the hole and looked around, shielding her eyes with her hand from the blinding white sunlight.

Miles and miles of desert seemed to stretch around her. From here, she could just make out the gas station of the small, one-horse town they'd passed, probably about five miles in the distance.

Pulling her body out fully and sliding off the burning metal side of the van, she crawled to the front driver's side and looked at Alice. The woman was unconscious. Mia opened the door and checked her, too. She was already waking, tossing her head from side to side as if in a fever dream. "No . . ." she murmured, "No . . ."

"Alice . . . what's going on? Alice . . . ?"

The CB radio's cord hung limp, and someone was speaking, the voice crackling with static. Mia ripped out the receiver, and smashed the radio with the butt of her gun. She reached into the cooler on the front passenger door and found cold water, sandwiches, and a few bruised apples. She took one of each.

"I'm sorry," Mia whispered to the woman, reaching into the center console and pulling out a pair of dark sunglasses.

She returned the gun to her waistband, put the sunglasses on, and strode defiantly into the desert, toward that little town, and more importantly, toward her home.

CHAPTER TWELVE

Ghost town.

As Mia stood in front of *Eddie's* Gas Station, scarfing down her sandwich—not that she was hungry, but because she didn't want to carry it anymore and wasn't sure when she'd next get to eat—she realized that getting home was not going to be as easy as she'd thought.

She pounded on the door for the tenth time, then looked forlornly at the *CLOSED* sign in the window and spun to take in the rest of her surroundings.

The house across the street didn't look any better. It was practically swallowed by vegetation, and its rusted corrugated roof had caved in. The only car in the driveway was half of one-- the carcass of an old Chevy so rusty, it probably couldn't even be used for parts.

She walked over to it and peered through the boards covering the front window. Through the darkness, she made out the floor and peeling wallpaper—but that was all. The place had been thoroughly cleaned out. No one had been there in years.

There was no one in town at all.

Then she looked down the road, the way she'd come, toward Dallas. The heat radiated from the blacktop, blurring the road ahead. The road was perfectly straight, flanked by nothing but vast expanses of dusty ground, skeletal creosote bushes and distant mountains. Overhead, buzzards circled.

She looked up at them, shielding her eyes from the sun. *Not today guys,* she thought. *Or at least, I hope.*

She had to move. Even with the radio smashed, the police would soon be onto her. She didn't have time to linger.

She took a step toward Dallas. An old thermometer at the front of the station had proclaimed 105 degrees. She felt every degree as she meandered down the road, unsure what she should do.

Pausing, she closed her eyes, picturing a map of the area in her head. This was the right way to go, for sure, but would she be able to make it in time? Or at all? In the van, they hadn't passed a car in ages. And the town, before this gas station, had probably been twenty miles

81

away. She couldn't walk that far. Not with half a bottle of water to her name. Not in this heat.

But she had no choice. Not unless someone came by and picked her up.

And who would do that, with her wearing this bright orange jumpsuit? They'd have to be suicidal. She'd even seen signs outside the prison, as they'd left: *PRISON AREA—DO NOT PICK UP HITCHHIKERS.*

About a mile down the road, as she walked, her back to the setting sun, she spied a sign that said, *Canyon River Campground.* An arrow pointed the way south, winding downwards into a slot canyon. In the distance, among the haze, she thought she saw something dark and shiny and manmade.

Well, if there was a river down there, she was all for it. If nothing, she could at least refill her water bottle for the journey so she wouldn't die of thirst.

As she walked, she thought of Chloe, and picked up the pace. Her only saving grace was that Wilson Andrews was a cocky son of a bitch. He thought there was no hope for her. He probably wouldn't expect she could escape. So he probably thought he could take his time, killing Chloe.

But he wouldn't take too long. Once word got out that she'd escaped, which would probably be a few hours at most . . . all bets were off.

She needed to get back to Dallas. Soon.

The sun was sinking ever faster, though. It was getting cooler, and soon, it'd be downright cold. If she didn't get back to Dallas by tonight, she could be too late.

By the time she reached the mouth of the canyon, where the road cut between two vertical cliffsides that were nearly perpendicular to the ground, she was running, despite the blisters on her feet from her cheap, prison-appointed sneakers.

She heard the sound of what she thought was wind, rushing through the narrow channel, but as she drew closer, she realized it was the river. She realized the black thing she'd seen was a shiny Ford F150, with a trailer attached to it. It was what Aidan would've called "A pretty sweet set-up." He'd always had pick-up truck dreams, and fantasized about heading out on the open road, no responsibilities, no worries.

I need that truck, she thought, biting her lip.

Crouching behind a boulder, she watched from afar as a tall, older man with white hair, cargo shorts, and a fishing vest, came out of the trailer with a couple of beers in his hands. Completely oblivious to her, he headed for the river.

Quietly, making sure she was alone, she crept to the side of the road where the truck was parked and peered in the front window. It was definitely nice inside, clean and sleek—probably still with that new-car smell. Of course, no key in the ignition.

Sighing, she took the gun out of her bag and crept toward the river, where she'd seen the man disappear. He was there, on the bank, with a younger man in a backward baseball cap. They were tossing lines into the narrow river, talking and laughing, something about the Dallas Cowboys and their chances this year, their backs to her.

Suddenly, a dog started barking. It was only then that she noticed the Golden Retriever beside them.

Alerted by the sound, the men turned and caught sight of her.

The dog barked some more, than rushed up and stopped short, begging to be petted.

Oh, gosh, he's cute, she thought, willing him away. She had work to do.

"Hey, Gunther!" one of the men said, looking toward her. "Get back here."

The dog did as it was told. Her decision made for her, she pulled out her gun and pointed it at them. "Men, I'm sorry to disturb your trip," she said, advancing toward them as they raised their hands in surrender. "But I really need the keys to your truck. And . . . I'd be really grateful if you could detach the trailer."

The men looked at each other. Then, the older man reached into his pocket and came forward. He was holding the keys up for her. "S-sure," he said gently, so gently, he reminded her of her dad.

He tossed the keys at her feet.

She looked at them, almost wishing he'd be a jerk about it. Maybe it'd make this easier.

"Your phones, too. I need your phones," she said, still holding the gun as she picked up the keys. "Unlock them for me, will you?"

Both men took out their phones and tossed them as well. As she did, she noticed the older man was sweating, trembling.

Her heart thudded with regret. He looked like anyone's grandfather, a sweet, kind old man who'd give the shirt off his back to anyone, and not because a gun was pointed at him.

"I'm sorry. I don't want to do this," she babbled. "But I . . . I'm not going to hurt you. I just need your truck."

Then the older man went to the trailer and unhitched it for her. "If you don't mind me saying, Miss, you look like you've had a bad time of it."

She felt too guilty for having to do this to them, so she said nothing.

"There's a first aid kit in the glove compartment," he added.

She realized he was looking at her forehead. She touched it and realized she had a bloody trail, now so dry it was scraping off, stretching from her temple to her chin. "I'm okay."

"Where are you headed?" he continued, now sounding a bit more relaxed.

"Home," she murmured as he finished lifting the latches.

He wiped his hands on his cargo shorts. "Should be good to go. We packed some things in the back, though . . . things we haven't unloaded. Some sleeping bags and some food."

She motioned with her gun. "You can take them out."

He shook his head. "No. For you."

Her lower lip trembled. Here she was, an escaped convict, robbing them, leaving them alone in this desolate area, and they were *helping her?*

She didn't have time to argue, though. The guards could be right on her tail. She opened the door and climbed in. As she did, she said, "Thank you. I promise. I'll treat your truck gentle. Like a newborn kitten. You'll get it back."

The two men just stared at her, astonished.

"Please," she said. "Keep fishing. I hope you catch a lot. I didn't mean to spoil your father-son trip."

She slammed the door, dug the key in the ignition and peeled off, out of the canyon, leaving a cloud of dust in her wake.

*

By nightfall, she was burning rubber down the remote road through the canyon. It was so remote, even GPS didn't work out here, but driving in an easterly direction, away from the sun, which was now just

84

a thin swath of light in her rear-view mirror, she knew she was going the right way.

Insects pelted the front windshield as she grabbed one of the phones out of the cup holder and dialed the number with one hand. The phone rang and rang, and for a moment, she thought it'd go to voicemail.

Then, there was a click, and the muted rumble of conversation. Over the din, a voice said, "Hello?"

"David? Is that you?"

"Wh—" A pause. "Mia? Mia?"

"Yeah, it's me."

"What the hell? Where are you? I just saw it on the news. Don't tell me it's true. Did you just break out of jail?"

Shit. So only six hours had passed, and the news had already gotten out that she was on the lam. "You know why. I had to. Did you get my message?"

"I did but . . . hell! Mia," he said in a warning tone. "Those guards . . . what did you do?"

"Nothing! It was an accident, and—"

"You need to turn yourself in before you make this worse for yourself. Your photo's being plastered everywhere and the dragnet's only gonna get tighter. What the hell were you thinking?"

"I told you. Chloe's in danger."

He let out a breath of air that hissed through his teeth. "She's not. She's absolutely safe. I assure you."

"You told Pembroke?"

"It doesn't matter," he said in a smaller voice.

That's a no. Of course. He doesn't trust you anymore. "David . . ." she began, searching desperately for something to prove herself.

"No. Listen. The police have this. They are keeping tabs on her. They get that her kidnapper is still out there, and that Sara might be, too. So they moved her family to a place outside of town. She's being well cared for."

"I need to know where she's living now. Can you get me her file?"

"No. Absolutely not."

"David . . . please."

"I'm going to hang up now."

"David . . . She's going to die." Mia wrapped her fingers tighter on the steering wheel. She knew him well enough to know that he had that same bug inside him—he simply couldn't look away when someone was about to get hurt. "How will you feel if something happens to her, and you did nothing?"

Mia gnawed on the inside of her cheek, waiting for his answer. Finally, he said, "Even if I wanted to, I couldn't get you that stuff. Not without everyone else finding out. Pembroke would ream me."

"So you didn't tell him, then."

A snort. "Of course not."

"Why didn't you tell Pembroke?" she asked, but she already knew the answer. He was afraid to. Afraid of being labeled paranoid, like she'd been. She just wanted him to be a man and admit it.

"I'm not supposed to be in touch with you, Mia. You know that."

She banged her hand on the steering wheel. "David. This is a matter of life and death. I had no one else to call."

"You shouldn't be calling me," he mumbled. "Look. I'm not at home. I'm on a date. I've got to go. Don't call me again. Any help I give you could wind up getting us both caught. I can't risk that."

"No, no wait—" she blurted, afraid he'd hung up. When she didn't hear the click, she said, "You know Zippy's Auto Repair, on the corner of Eighth and Walnut?"

A pause. "The one that closed down last month? What about it?"

"Yeah. The night drop box. For the keys. Someone busted it open, remember?"

"Yeah. I remember."

"If you leave the files in there, I can get them there. Tonight."

"Tonight!" There was a sorrowful laugh. "Girl. I want to help. I really do. But I just told you, I'm on a date. I don't know if I can--"

"You're on a date? Really, David?"

A sigh. "Pembroke—"

"He doesn't have to know," she said. He was always one to play by the book. He'd probably never even so much as rolled through a stop sign in his life. She knew this was hard for him. *Lying* about anything, even if it was for good, was hard for him. "And Chloe is in trouble."

There was a long pause. He mumbled a curse under his breath. "All right. I'll see what I can do."

"Thanks, David. I owe you one."

"I know you do. But Mia?"

She swallowed, hoping he wasn't going to get mushy on her. "Yeah?"

"Take care of yourself. I'm sorry about . . . well . . . you know."

86

Mia smiled. She'd been somewhat bitter after what he'd said at the trial. But she couldn't blame him. He was a good man. He only spoke the truth, as he saw it.

He may have thought she was paranoid. He may have thought she'd taken the thing with Ellis Horvath a little too far. But David was helping her, at least.

And that meant he didn't think she was a cold-blooded murderer.

She ended the call and drove on, until she could see the city lights in the distance. She yawned, and realized she hadn't slept in over twenty-four hours. It would take a while for David to go into headquarters and get her the file, anyway, so there wasn't much she could do, now.

She navigated to the side of the road. Climbing out of the truck, she dropped the tailgate and looked inside. Sure enough, there was a cooler and a couple of sleeping bags and blankets.

They'd probably be looking for this truck by now, though, and they could probably trace the phone. It was best to leave them. Dallas was close. Her experience in investigation told her that it was best never to hold on to any of that for too long. She needed to keep switching up, to move on.

She packed up a bag with food, and hiked into the desert. On a craggy bluff, she found a bottle of Coke and took a drink of it, then spread out the bag on the ground and laid out, looking up at the stars. Here, away from the city lights, it was a virtual night carnival, the wide expanse of sky full of millions and millions of stars.

Beautiful. Even when everything goes wrong, the world can still be so beautiful.

It was that pleasant thought that stopped the thoughts from madly whirring in her head, brought peace to her mind, and gradually lulled her to sleep.

CHAPTER THIRTEEN

Mia was at the playground in her neighborhood, with Kelsey. Kelsey giggled and ran ahead, going straight for the swings. She, like Mia when she'd been a kid, could spend hours on those swings, trying to touch the sky.

"Look at me, Mom! Look at me!" she shouted as she went on and began pumping her legs furiously.

Mia smiled, happy to be there with her daughter. As much as she wanted to grab her and hug her tight, she wanted her to be free, to be happy.

"Push me, Mom! Push me higher!"

Mia got behind her and began to push. But the second she pushed her away, Kelsey disappeared.

Now, suddenly, Mia was sitting on a swing, in the playground outside her old elementary school. It was one of those old-school, half domes, high in the center, and she was there, with her class, as most of the kids climbed on the monkey bars or the jungle gym, or went up and down on the seesaw. They ran about, shrieking in glee, their laughter echoing in Mia's ears.

But Mia had always preferred the swings. She wanted to fly.

Grasping the chains, the plastic seat pressed against her backside, she backed up as far as she could go. Then she jumped up onto the seat and flew forward, stretching her legs out in front of her, then pulling them back to get momentum.

Wearing her best dress and Mary Janes, she leaned back, pumping her legs, trying to touch the sky.

"Higher!" she said, pumping more furiously.

A hand at her back pushed, giving her the extra help she needed.

"Oh, higher!" she giggled, her hair flapping into her face. "Push me higher!"

It was only when she came back down that she realized the ground was closer. So close, she was afraid her legs would hit it.

She snatched them up again, but realized it wasn't the ground beneath her. She studied it, sure her eyes were playing tricks on her, that in the blur of her movement, she'd seen it wrong.

But no.

It was a big, black void.

An icy tendril of terror seized her and she looked up, only to realize that the playground was empty. All of her friends had disappeared. Only echoes of their laughing voices remained.

The playground wasn't just empty, though. All of the playground equipment—the dome-shaped climber, the spinning carousel . . . it was all melting away, turning gooey and black and charred, the ruins of some horrible disaster.

She looked over each shoulder. The playground seemed to shrink in on her, the murk growing closer, threatening to crush her. The dark spaces of the trees around her seemed too near, reaching out to grab her.

Mia kept kicking, desperate to stay out of the blackness. But then she realized that she still had that hand at her back, pushing her ever higher.

She turned, slowly, afraid of what she might see.

But there was no one there.

When she turned back, though, just as she'd reached the top of the back arc and was preparing to come down, she saw it.

A shadowy figure, directly in front of her.

Beckoning to her.

It opened its maw, black lips separating to reveal a pair of serpent tongues, uncoiling for her arrival. *Come to me, Mia . . .*

She sat up, heard pounding, just as she was about to fly into its arms, and looked around.

The sun was just preparing to rise over the distant hills. The silent desert all around her, she took in a breath of the last of the cold, night air. Letting it out, a cloud of it puffed up around her face. She grasped her steadily beating heart, willing it to quiet down.

You're safe. They haven't gotten you yet.

Jumping up, she rolled her sleeping bag and looked around, trying to orient herself. She took a few more sips of Coke and headed in the direction of the city.

About a half hour later, she came to civilization. First, sprawling ranch houses, widely interspersed, and then, a main road. She walked

89

along it, trying to remain inconspicuous, until she came to a supermarket. It was still early, though. She didn't have her phone, but she estimated it was probably before six in the morning.

There were only two cars in the lot—an old-model Porsche, a little banged-up, and a black Jeep Cherokee.

Her stomach roiled. She hated the thought of stealing from another person, but she had no choice.

Looking around to make sure there was nobody watching her, she tried the door to the Jeep.

It opened. Quickly, she slipped inside and closed the door, then bent low beneath the dashboard, trying to find the wires. It'd been a long time since she'd been shown how to hotwire a car, and it definitely wasn't on the schedule at Quantico—her first partner had once been a gang-banger who'd lifted his share of cars in his day--but it was a lesson she'd never forgotten.

After her first couple of tries, the Jeep's engine purred to life. Sighing with relief, she shifted into drive and eased out of the parking lot, trying her best not to call attention to herself.

Once she reached the outside of the city, though, she floored the gas pedal, headed toward Zippy's Auto Repair. She only hoped that David would come through for her and do as he'd promised.

Chloe, she thought. *I hope that I am not too late. Please be all right.*

CHAPTER FOURTEEN

Route forty-six, south of Dallas, was dying.

Once a busy place, full of bustling stores and too much traffic, now, it was full of empty storefronts, all with FOR SALE and AVAILABLE signs in the windows. The massive indoor shopping mall had been demolished, years ago, and the people just didn't come anymore. The interstate had taken people off the road, directing them just south of the area, and now, it was no longer convenient. Besides, people didn't shop and those ma and pa shops anymore—they went to Target and Wal Mart and the other big box stores for the things they needed, or ordered online from Amazon.

So even though it was rush hour, when Mia pulled to the side of the road, just before Zippy's Auto Repair, she didn't have the cover of other cars to conceal her appearance. She craned her neck and peered toward the once-white, now dim gray building with its six closed garage bays.

No cars.

Nothing. No activity whatsoever.

Good, she thought, looking around. Across the empty four-lane road, at the old Fuddruckers, a homeless person wheeled a shopping cart absently around the corner, disappearing behind the dumpsters. A few birds fought over some scraps in the parking lot of the shuttered Sears. Other than that, she was alone.

At least, she hoped.

There was still the thought in the back of her mind that David, goody-two-shoes that he was, had betrayed her. Ratted her out to Pembroke, and they were now waiting for her to show up so they could put her back in prison.

But she couldn't think about that now. She had no choice but to trust him.

She pounded the gas and pulled into the lot of Zippy's, focused on just one thing—the overnight drop box between bays three and four. As she pulled up, she noted the same thing she'd seen earlier—the lock had been removed. Now, the OVERNIGHT DROP BOX: CAR KEYS HERE was faded from the sun.

Coming to an abrupt stop in front of it, she jumped out of the car, gnawing on her bottom lip and saying a little prayer. *Please, God. Please, David. Please have done what I asked you to do.*

She approached the box, looking for something. A hint of paper from the file, poking out. Not seeing anything, she lunged forward and the sinking feeling already inside her grew as she opened the top of the box and saw nothing. She reached inside, feeling to the bottom, but grasped only air.

Dammit, David, she thought, biting her tongue as she looked around. *I thought I could trust you.*

Now, she half-expected the police to come screaming around the corner at any moment. Had he set her up, or decided to blow her off?

She was just about to rush back to her car when there was a low rumble. Suddenly, the door of garage bay number six, half-hidden in the shadows behind the waiting room area that protruded from the front of the building, began to roll up.

It stopped halfway and David, dressed in his normal workday suit, peeked out. He motioned her in. "In here."

She hesitated for a moment, then followed, ducking under the door. "David, I told you—"

"Just shut up and listen, for once in your life," he said. "You're not my superior officer anymore, so you don't get to tell me what to do, all right?"

She supposed that was true. Her eyes adjusted to the dark, and she looked around. He'd parked his car inside the bay. She had to wonder how long he'd been waiting for her. "Fine, but you could get in trouble."

"Yeah, yeah, yeah. And I had to miss dropping my kid off at school today, too. Life's a bitch. What else is new?" he said, opening his trunk. Then he looked back at her. "You look like hell, North. What you been up to?"

She smiled, in spite of herself. He could always make her smile, even during the worst of times.

His trunk was just as clean as he kept his desk—everything in its place, with military precision. She saw the manila folder at once, about an inch thick. He handed it to her. "It's a copy. I spent an hour at the Xerox machine last night. Enjoy."

"Thanks," she said, opening it and paging through it carefully, so that she wouldn't drop any of the loose papers. The second page she came to, she found the address she was looking for.

"*Twenty-six Pine Top Trail,*" she read. "Do you know where that is?"

He nodded. "North of town. I should know. Like I said, I've been there three times this week." He shook his head. "It's secure, Mia. Nothing's gonna get to her, there. No one even knows about it."

"Andrews knows. He has ways of finding things out."

He shook his head. "Mia. You know how this sounds, right? Andrews is a respected member of society. He's not going to go rogue and try to murder a girl in broad—"

"He's sick. I'm telling you. He might have been an upstanding member of society, but when he met Sara, something in him snapped. And I know it's nothing like what the profilers say, but I promise you . . . he visited me in prison. And he told me he was going to get her. He likes doing this. Playing this game. It's all about power to him."

David shook his head. "It sounds—"

"Paranoid?" she said, repeating the word he'd said at the trial.

His eyes drooped with remorse. "Yeah—about that . . ."

"Look, David. I know what it looked like. And if I were in your place, if my partner started spouting off those things about Wilson Andrews, I'd probably think she was crazy, too." She sighed. "So I don't hold what happened at the trial against you. You called it as you saw it. That's what you had to do."

He let out a deep breath. "Yeah, but . . ."

She backed away. "I'd love to stay and chat, but I've got somewhere to be." She held up the folder. "Thanks for this, David. You're a pal."

She was just about to turn back to her car when he said, "Hey, wait."

She stopped, and he reached into the trunk and pulled out a backpack, holding it up for her. "Here. Take this. There's a change of clothes, some food, other things I thought you'd need."

Mia took it, and opened her mouth to say how grateful she was, but then closed it. She knew David well enough to know that this was his peace offering. He might have thought she was paranoid, but he'd been through a lot with her, enough to know she wouldn't say something unless she absolutely believed it. He trusted her.

"And this," he said, handing her a white plastic shopping bag. "I picked those up this morning. It's a couple of burner phones."

Now, she couldn't resist. It seemed that he'd thought of everything. "Thank you."

"Don't mention it," he said, heading to the back of his SUV. "Just . . . Mia. I know you didn't want me to be here, but remember. I put my ass on the line for you. So I strongly advise you to resist using those phones to call your family."

She nodded, looking away. It was, in fact, the first thing she'd thought about. "All right."

The first thing she had to do, anyway, was get to Pine Top Trail. If her intuition was right, there was a good chance Andrews was already staking it out, so there wasn't a moment to lose. Any longer, and he might learn that she'd escaped. Maybe he already knew.

She rushed toward the open garage door.

"And Mia?"

She stopped short and looked back at her partner.

"Take care of yourself."

Mia nodded. "Will do."

CHAPTER FIFTEEN

Andrews watched the house with all the excitement of a kid on Christmas morning.

Sitting in his hiding spot, he waited. It was an ingenious spot, considering—luck so had it that the temporary Braxton family home backed up to acres of forest which abutted the local highway on the opposite side. He'd parked there, and crept through the forest on foot. There was a shed in the back corner of the house that had multiple doors and no padlock. He'd easily squirreled himself away inside the space in the middle of the night, and now here he waited, a little dizzy from the fertilizer fumes, eating a Snickers bar, half-melted from the already oppressive heat for ten in the morning.

The house may have only been temporary refuge, but the police had provided the Braxtons with a pretty sweet set-up. A nice place in a quiet residential neighborhood, north of Dallas. Big inground pool with a cabana. Hot tub. Nice deck, overlooking the sprawling, lush-lawned backyard. The lawn was covered with toys from the girl's little brother, a toy xylophone, a couple of buckets and shovels for the turtle-shaped sandbox. Floating on the pool were a couple of giant blow-up unicorn floats. They hadn't been outside much, since arriving, and who could blame them?

Gradually, though, they'd been coming outside, taking advantage of this big, secluded yard, and the warm summer sun. They'd been putting their trauma behind them. Trying to move on.

A mistake, really.

The police had already gone lax with their surveillance, considering this morning, they were nowhere to be found.

Yet another mistake.

But he planned to take full advantage of both of those unfortunate circumstances.

He breathed in the morning air and waited for her to appear.

Waited for her, in all her blonde, tanned glory, to show up, wearing that little yellow bikini. He got hard, just thinking of her. She wasn't what made his heart beat—Sara was, of course—but the two of them,

95

together? They shared secrets. And he couldn't risk that she might suddenly remember what happened.

He'd been worried before.

That was what started all this. Only a year ago, he'd been fine. Oh, he'd had his manias, his obsessions—porn, hunting, scotch—but all those were normal male obsessions. Erica was the typical nagging wife who liked to spend his money. His kids were constantly sapping his patience. Work was . . . well, work. He used his vices to get away from the stresses in his life.

And life was pretty good.

Until Sara.

He'd met her at a pool party for an associate and family friend, Caleb Waverly. Their families had grown up together. April seventh, at 4:35 PM. He remembered the moment with absolute clarity, because at that moment, his world had tilted slightly on its axis, changing forever.

He hadn't much cared for the schmoozing, not like the rest of the Andrews clan. He'd gone to their annual party once, years ago, and Sara had only been six or seven. A baby. But at 4:35 PM, he walked out of the sliding glass door from the Waverly's kitchen, expecting nothing more than a boring barbecue, a few burgers and dogs, some beer, and inane conversation.

That was when he caught sight of her, standing on the diving board in her pink bikini, ready to dive in.

He was in love.

Until that moment, he never knew what the word was. But it hit him, like they say in the movies, right between the eyes.

He'd gotten Erica a glass of wine, nearly tripping over himself because he couldn't tear his eyes away from the girl doing laps in the pool. He'd nearly spilled the wine on his wife, he'd been so entranced. He'd listened with one ear to all the banter, fudged a bunch of introductions, all the while positioning himself to get a better look at the goddess. All he could see—all he *wanted* to see—from that point on, was the gorgeous woman in the pool.

Then, as if he was in a fantasy, she pulled herself out of the pool and, still dripping, walked toward him as he stumbled his way through a conversation with his host. As she did, she became even more of a vision than he'd first imagined. Full lips, long, waist-length blonde hair, a perfect ten body. And she was staring at him with eyes that said, *Take me now.*

And then everything came crashing down.

She gave Caleb Waverly a kiss on the cheek and said, "I'm going to go inside and get changed, Daddy. Chloe'll be here in five."

That was when he realized he was in trouble.

The rest of the party, he watched the two girls, knowing he was losing it. Knowing the carefully woven fabric of his life—classy upbringing, loving family, good job-- was now slowly unravelling. Of course she was just a kid. He could tell that, now, by the way she splashed her friend, by the way she giggled. Just a kid.

He tried to put her out of his mind. Tried, and failed. For months, it was all he thought about. And then, he decided he could control it no longer. He needed to give into the desire. Somehow.

He'd watch them, almost blatantly. Oh, certainly, he'd disguise himself, but anyone who looked twice would probably see the lust in his eyes. When he wasn't working, he'd follow the girls around, like a lost puppy. Sara, for all her beauty, had been oblivious, but Chloe had been different. Once, he'd followed them to Water World, the local water park. He'd watched them in their bikinis, prancing about, splashing each other, and enjoying the slides, growing harder and harder by the second.

But then, Chloe had noticed him, spying on them from behind the gate. *Ew! Dirty old man!* She'd cried, causing a commotion and making everyone in the vicinity turn.

He'd run, jumped into his car and sped off, narrowly escaping detection. He'd driven to an abandoned park outside of town and beat off in the front seat of his car.

That had been a close one.

But he couldn't help it. When Sara was in his line of sight, nothing else mattered. He simply couldn't trust himself to act right. She was easily the most gorgeous woman on earth. All he had to do was think about her, and he'd tremble with longing. It only got worse and worse, until he knew he had to possess her.

And so he had. Easy, really. She'd gone with him willingly, because she'd thought of him as a family friend.

The rest of the world didn't understand.

They didn't understand what he and Sara shared. They never would.

Then the police started to interview Chloe about the disappearance of her best friend. Chloe, the smart one. And he was afraid of what she

97

might say. He'd watch the interviews on television, and knew she was close to piecing things together. If she made the connection, his life was over.

So a few weeks later, he'd taken her, too. Easily. With such a smart mouth, he'd thought she'd put up more of a fight. But she didn't.

It was almost a disappointment. In fact, he wanted to get rid of Chloe from the moment he took her. She was a pain in the ass. Not sweet and docile, like Sara. His love. His *life*.

But she was out, now. And though she had a selective memory, though he'd worn a mask each time he visited her in that basement, she was smart. Eventually, she'd put two and two together.

And he couldn't let that happen.

Moments later, the door opened, and she appeared. He sighed with longing. Pain in the ass or not, she'd been fun. He missed their time together.

She wasn't the same Chloe, though. She was wearing shorts and a t-shirt, and her hair was a mess, as if she'd just woken up. Maybe that was his doing, but it didn't bother him. Young girls needed to learn, eventually, that life wasn't all sunshine and roses. That happiness was finite, and sometimes, people had to suffer so that others might thrive.

He watched her go down to the pool, then sit on the edge, tipping her toes into the deep end.

Little Bird, Little Bird, he thought, rising from his crouching position. He wound the thick length of rope tightly around his hands. *It is time I silence your song.*

He took a single step toward her place at the edge of the pool. Yes, this would be easy. She was facing away from him. Just a few more steps and—

Suddenly, he heard the sound of tires screeching on the pavement. This quiet residential area didn't get much traffic, and rarer still were people driving like a bat out of hell. The police? Quickly, he backed away, into his hiding spot behind an old, mossy lawnmower, checking behind him to make sure his escape route was still clear.

Then he saw the Jeep, rounding the corner, skidding to a stop in front of the house.

Curiously, he watched, as a slim, petite woman threw open the door.

Ah, interesting.

He'd always known that Mia North was one smart cookie. Another big pain in the ass, but a smart cookie, definitely.

Unfortunately, she didn't know one crucial thing about the city she'd grown up in: The Andrews family could do no wrong.

A shame. No, not at all fair. But true.

But despite that one flaw, she was resourceful. Those who thought she'd play by the rules while incarcerated, be a good girl and hope she could earn brownie points that would lead her to an early release . . . they'd underestimated her. Just like they underestimated him.

"Good for you," he whispered to himself with a smile. He liked the challenge, anyway. His family loved competition.

He also loved proving people wrong.

And he would do it again. Happily.

Mia had thought he wouldn't get away with this.

She has no idea how wrong she is, he thought, throwing open the back door to the shed and slipping out into the forest. When he was there, he pulled out a burner phone and dialed 9-1-1, smiling from ear to ear, exhilarated. *Okay, Agent North. You want to play with me? Let the games begin.*

CHAPTER SIXTEEN

Mia cursed under her breath as she pulled up to the ranch house located in a wooded section of Pine Top Trail.

Whoever had selected this location as a hiding spot for the Braxton family clearly needed to learn a thing or two. If Mia had done the choosing, she would've picked a bigger neighborhood, closer to the police station. And she definitely wouldn't have picked a house that backed up to the woods.

Plus? No police cars out front. Not even plain-clothes. No one.

So much for the Dallas Police taking care of things. Someone was definitely dropping the ball with this one.

Everything looked okay. Quiet. But Mia knew that with Wilson Andrews, appearances were very deceiving.

Her tires squealed underneath her as she braked hard in front of the house, throwing open the door and stepping out even before the car had come to a full stop. She rushed onto the porch, past the WELCOME sign and potted flowers, and banged furiously on the door.

A few moments later, a woman answered. She was probably in her mid-forties, bouncing a toddler with a chocolate moustache on her hip. There was concern on her face as she scanned Mia from head to toe. "I know you . . ."

Mia nodded. She knew her, too. They'd never met, but Mia had seen her on the news, begging for her daughter's safe return home. Though she still had Chloe's striking looks, the woman looked a lot older now, her bobbed hair pushed back in a headband to reveal a face full of worry creases. "Yes, you do, Mrs. Braxton?"

"Yes, I'm Ruth Braxton. And what is this—"

"Is Chloe here?"

The woman looked over her shoulder, then back at her. "Who are you?"

"I'm FBI," she said. This was where she'd pull out her credentials, if she still had them. "I'm –"

"And the FBI wears orange prison jumpsuits with DOJ painted on them, now, huh?" she asked in confusion.

"No. Mrs. Braxton. I'm Mia North, the agent who found your daughter. I—"

The woman gasped. "I heard something about you. I don't watch the news anymore. Not since—you know." She set her baby down and told him to go off to the playroom. Then she stared hard at Mia. "What's going on?"

"Look. You know the man who took Chloe is still at large."

She nodded. "Yes, but the police said they had a suspect—"

"I don't know about that. But I know who the killer is. And I have reason to believe—"

"Reason?" She held up a hand and stared at her as if she was insane. "Wait. I heard this before. You were insistent that the kidnapper was that senator, weren't you?"

"It is. It's Wilson Andrews. I know it." Mia took a gulp of air and let it out. "Yes, I know it sounds crazy. But if you just—"

"You went after that other guy, too, didn't you? You thought he was stalking you. He was completely innocent, and yet you didn't want to believe it. And you killed him. That's what the paper said," she said, scanning the street, probably for the police cars that were supposed to be watching her. "Look. I'm glad you brought Chloe back to us. But you need to step away. Now."

"No. You don't understand. Wilson Andrews is afraid Chloe's going to speak. And he has access to the police. He's after her, and it won't be hard for him to find her here. You need to leave this house and get away from here. As far as you can. *Please*."

She reached into the pocket of her loose sleeveless cardigan and pulled out a phone. "I think you need to go. I'm calling the police."

"No, pleas—"

She froze when she heard it, in the distance but growing louder.

Sirens. The police were coming.

She backed away, nearly tripping over a potted plant as she did. "Please," she called to her. "You have to get out of here. You have to—"

"Mom? Who's that?" a voice from inside the house called. Through a window, Mia could just make out a slim silhouette, standing in the screen door near the back of the house. Chloe.

She didn't want to let the girl out of her sight.

But she had no choice. She took off, running, and it was only when she reached the street that she saw the police cars, speeding down the road, toward her.

She jumped into the Jeep and tried to start it again, already pressing on the gas to gun it forward.

But the engine simply sputtered and died.

She tried it again. Same result. Flooded.

"No," she bit out, watching the police car coming closer.

Grabbing David's backpack, she pulled herself out of the Jeep. She backed up, racing down the street, away from them. That was when she saw another police car, coming from the opposite direction, heading straight for her. She froze, looking around. Then she raced between two of the houses with thick, bushy landscaping.

At first, she crouched near a whirring air-conditioning, wondering what to do. No, they'd come after her. Find her. She had to run. Fast.

Making a quick decision, she pulled open a gate to the neighbor's house, and raced across the lawn, looking for somewhere to hide. No . . . she couldn't hide. She was a wanted escaped felon. As soon as Mrs. Braxton told the police she'd been here, they'd set out a perimeter. Fan out, searching for her, leave no stone unturned.

She had to run away from here, as far and as fast as she could. Now.

She heard the police cars skidding to a stop, their sirens roaring. Shouts. Commotion.

Keeping down low, heart thudding in her chest, she headed past the swing set in the back of the neighboring property, keeping her eyes open for the police. She darted from bush to compost bin to picnic table, using them for cover until the back fence, bordering the thick woods, was in sight.

As she stood up to make a dash for it, a brindle pit bull barked at her, snarling and snapping its jaws. She let out a yelp and fell back onto her rear end, ready for it to attack.

But it was on the other side of the chain-link fence.

It couldn't hurt her. But it would definitely alert the police to her presence.

Checking over her shoulder, she scrambled to her feet and raced for the back fence. She reached it and catapulted over it, landing on her back in a pile of dead leaves. Head foggy, vision twisting, she forced herself up and took off, only stopping for breath when she was hidden behind a tree.

She looked down at her clothes. *Damn orange. They'll spot me a mile away.*

Checking behind her, she quickly unbuttoned the jumpsuit, pulling it down to her hips. She opened the backpack and pulled out a dark Led Zeppelin t-shirt and a pair of jeans. Classic David. Lifting her butt and wiggling out of the suit, she slipped the change of clothes on. A little roomy, but better and more inconspicuous than that orange monstrosity.

Inside the backpack, she also found a trucker's cap and sunglasses. David had thought of everything, providing her with a nice disguise. Piling her hair up, she slipped the cap over her head and donned the sunglasses. It wouldn't make her invisible to the authorities, but it would help.

She felt in the pocket of the backpack and pulled out a set of car keys, alone with a note: *If you need a car, I parked a blue Honda at the junkyard at 11th and Chestnut. You can take the bus there.*

She smiled. He really had thought of everything.

She went through the rest of the things he'd given her: the phones, more clothes, a few granola bars, some Power Ade, a toothbrush and toothpaste. There was also a wallet filled with about a hundred dollars in cash. Sliding that into her back pocket, she listened. The sirens had stopped, but she could hear shouting. They'd be cordoning off the area, soon, looking for her. And maybe they'd be so interested in finding Mia that they wouldn't be keeping an eye on Chloe.

Maybe she just made it all the easier for Andrews to make his move.

Shuddering at the thought, she pushed against the trunk of the tree and stood. Keeping down low, she moved parallel to the back line of the property, until she came to the Braxton's temporary abode. She spied a large shed in the corner of the property, its door slightly open.

Nice move, guys, she thought, creeping over to it, careful to make sure no police were nearby. As she stepped closer, she saw them, in the mud.

Footprints, belonging to a male's dress shoe, probably size eleven. Her suspicions aroused, curiosity piqued, she had to go farther.

Slowly opening the door, she peeked inside. The smell of the fertilizer made her eyes water. She picked through the junk and saw a few empty candy wrappers, but nothing else.

But even though there was very little evidence, she was sure of it. Wilson Andrews had been there.

And now she was more worried about Chloe than ever.

She heard the nearby creak of a gate opening. The police were nearby. As badly as she wanted to help Chloe, there was nothing she could do.

Turning, she escaped out the back door of the shed and took off into the forest. About a half-a mile later, she came to a street, flagged down an Amazon driver, and hitched a ride to the junkyard.

She needed to get somewhere safe to go over the files for the case and plan her next move.

CHAPTER SEVENTEEN

Mia drove David's blue Honda through town, trying to determine what to do.

What she didn't want to do was spend too much time out in the open. Even with her disguise, there was too much of a risk that someone could recognize her.

She pulled into the parking lot of a cheap motel, munched on a granola bar courtesy of her partner, and went through the files on Wilson Andrews and his victims.

She'd poured over these papers for weeks, when she first picked up this cold case, so she didn't expect to see anything new. Back then, she'd had her doubts that Wilson Andrews was the All-American, Golden Boy he made himself out to be. But now, gazing at the picture of him, she felt truly sick. He was handsome, dressed in his suit and tie, smiling, a look on his face that said, *You can trust me.*

The man she'd seen in the prison, a few days ago? He'd still had that same smile, but it was the words he said that made her skin crawl. *Appearances can be deceiving. You can't trust anyone.*

Again, she went through his bio. Forty-seven years old, born and bred in the University Park section of Dallas, a silver spoon firmly wedged in his gums. He'd gone to Rice, graduated with a degree in politics, *summa cum laude*. Joined the Navy, did a tour in Afghanistan. Ran on an independent ticket and got a staggering eighty-one percent of the vote. Championed for the rights of women and the demoralized. Everyone loved Wilson Andrews.

That he could even be tied to the disappearance of Sara Waverly was unthinkable. The fact that Chloe Braxton had been found in a building belonging to him, and that he'd gone there with bleach and other cleaning supplies, seemed lost on the prosecutors. *Not enough evidence to convict*, they'd said, adding, *Besides, it's Wilson Andrews!* The *Wilson Andrews! He's never done anything wrong!*

And it was because of that perception that people had been letting him slide, all of his life. Funny, most politicians seemed mired in scandal. It was almost expected of them. But Wilson Andrews had been able to sail through it all with a lily-white reputation . . . and Mia was pretty sure he'd committed the worst crime of any of them.

Sighing, she went to take a bite of her granola bar and realized it was a melted puddle of chocolate that had dribbled from its wrapper, all over her hand. Licking it off, she closed the file and stared out at the haze of heat on the road ahead of her.

A man like Wilson Andrews needed to be stopped before he hurt anyone else.

And if she was already considered a criminal for something she didn't do, maybe she should go ahead and earn that sentence.

She shivered in the late day sunshine. In prison, they were probably being led down to the cafeteria for dinner. She could almost imagine Shilah, saying over her shoulder, "Dammit, meatloaf again?" Then she'd go and eat Mia's portion, in addition to her own.

She almost smiled at the thought.

Then she thought about what her family would be doing, right now. They'd be coming home from their days, getting ready for dinner.

Mia always tried to be home for dinner, but it was Aidan who was the cook. He'd have his famous ribs—Kelsey's favorite— waiting for her, complete with cornbread and coleslaw. She'd come in after a long day and smell that mouthwatering aroma, wafting through the house. Kelsey would come running in stocking feet, jumping into her arms, peppering her face with kisses. And they'd all sit on the back deck, by the fire pit, and eat their meals, throwing the bones in the fire like cavemen.

She let out an uneasy breath, her lungs aching. No . . . it was her heart. It hurt so much that she wanted to scream.

She did it almost involuntarily, without being able to stop herself. Twenty minutes later, she found herself on the street she lived on in University Park, slowing to a crawl when the house came into view.

It was a modest split-level, from the 1970s, but it was in a spectacular neighborhood with lots of mature trees and families with young children, and "it has good bones." That was what Aidan had said when they put in the offer on it. And indeed, it had. Over their past fifteen years of marriage, they'd spent a lot of time fixing it up, making it theirs. They'd painted it, put in a shed and sunroom, added the pool and basketball court out back, really putting their North family signature on it.

And now, she was less than a hundred yards from it, and she couldn't even walk through the front door.

She heard the sound of tires on the pavement, and shrunk down, low, into her seat, as a familiar car passed by.

Her heart lodged itself in her throat as she looked up and realized it was Aidan's car. She checked the time on the dash. After five. He was home from picking her up a little late. Maybe from basketball practice. Sad, she'd always been the one to keep Kelsey's schedule straight. Now, she had no idea what her daughter's days were like.

They were *right there,* and yet they might as well have been a million miles away.

She watched with longing as the doors of the sedan opened, and out slinked Kelsey, wearing her too-big basketball uniform—number seven—and carrying a bag that was bigger than she was, and sucking on a straw from a blue plastic cup. Probably a milkshake.

So she'd had a game. They always used to get milkshakes after a game.

Kelsey's head was down. Either the team had lost that game, or it was something else.

Why was her hair like that? Mia always did her hair in braids for a game, but now she had a messy ponytail hanging sadly on her shoulder. And that hot pink headband wasn't regulation. She'd likely gotten in trouble for wearing that. The division only allowed black or gray.

The lights of the car went off, and the driver's side door opened. Aidan stepped out, carrying a bag of DQ.

Mia winced. A milkshake was fine, but the other stuff? Yuck. How many times had they told Kelsey that stuff was poison? Probably a thousand. She had to wonder what he'd packed in her lunchbox. Probably those gummy things, which would be hell on her braces.

But Mia suppressed all those impulses. Braces, bad fast food, hot pink headbands . . . Who cared, really? It all seemed so inconsequential, now. Like trying to polish the deck of a sinking ship. Her family had other things on their minds, right now.

They were falling apart.

Besides, if they were eating poison, juggling knives, doing stupid, reckless things that would only give them more trouble . . . it was all her own fault.

Oblivious to her, the two people she loved most in the world headed toward the front door, Aidan saying something under his breath.

It sounded like he was reciting the rules of basketball to her. He sounded cross, like he was reprimanding her for dribbling the wrong way. That was odd. He never yelled, and he certainly didn't care if she did terribly at basketball. Not at all. He used to say, "Who cares if you win or lose! Just go out there and have fun!"

Her head hung lower. He dropped the keys and cursed loudly.

Mia swallowed. He never cursed, especially not in front of Kelsey.

They went inside, leaving the front door open. She watched, tilting this way and that in her chair as they went inside and the lights of the house went on. She saw them setting out the food on the kitchen table, Kelsey picking at the French fries that were once her favorite food, Aidan staring into space. They didn't speak. It was like they were just going through the motions, sleepwalking through their lives.

All because of her.

But she couldn't stay. She had to get somewhere away from them, somewhere the police wouldn't think to look for her.

She hardened her face, willing the tears not to come.

It didn't work. They came anyway. She started the car and pulled away, wiping the tears from her cheeks as she drove.

CHAPTER EIGHTEEN

Mia found a motel outside of town, the kind of place where they asked no questions.

That was exactly what she was looking for when she got her key from the manager and went to her room, number six, right by the vending machines. It was dark, with seventies décor, and it smelled like mothballs and old cigarettes.

There, she turned on the old chain chandelier and spread out her dinner under its amber glow, atop a laminated table that someone had carved SUCK THIS into, and a picture of a crudely drawn penis. She'd spent all the change David had given her, loading up on Andy Capp's Hot Fries and pretzels and Coke for dinner, wondering why she'd ever looked down upon Kelsey and Aidan's dinner choice.

This was prime dining, right here.

She opened up the folder again, wondering what new things she'd glean from it, and turned on the television set, looking for any news of her escape. Unsurprisingly, she was the top story. The anchor said, "Tonight, known murderer and former FBI agent Mia North is on the loose, after having escaped from a prison transfer, late last night. Suspect is considered armed and extremely dangerous."

"Armed." She almost laughed as she looked at her things. She'd left the gun that she'd gotten from the guards in the truck, by accident, when she'd headed out into the desert. *I can kill you with my Andy Capp's Hot Fries breath.*

"Suspect is also considered to be an expert at evading authorities, due to her former profession."

She shrugged. "Not exactly," she said. Sure, she knew more than the average person, but this being her first time and all, she'd just been making this up as she went along.

"Here's a photograph of Mia North. Anyone having seen her should call this number with tips."

A picture of her flashed on the screen. It was taken years ago, when she'd graduated from the FBI academy. Her hair had been shorter then, and darker. Maybe that was a good thing, that they didn't have anything more recent.

The news went on to other things, but that was all. And there was nothing about the commotion she'd caused earlier outside the Braxton residence. They'd probably called in the US Marshals to find her. Did they really have no leads at all on her? Or were they just being mum so that she'd let her guard down?

She opened up the folder and scanned it. Andrews had been there, in the Braxton's backyard. He seemed to like tempting fate, taunting and playing with people, which was why he'd visited her in prison to gloat.

She had a very good idea he'd return to the Braxton house.

But not while the police were there, swarming the place. He was crazy, but not suicidal. Was he?

She didn't think so.

At least, she hoped not.

She'd make her move tomorrow, when the police were gone. She'd hide there, in waiting, as long as it took. He'd come. He had to come.

After her feast, stomach churning, she went to the old, lumpy mattress, and curled up, trying to sleep. But sleep didn't come.

She kept thinking of her family, Aidan and Kelsey in that big house, missing her.

Tears flowed.

*

By two in the morning, she knew she'd never be able to fall asleep unless she took care of something. Quickly dressing, she got into the Honda and stole across town, into the University Park neighborhood. She pulled into the cul-de-sac at the end of the road and parked there, then carefully sneaked up to the back door, staying in the shadows. Reaching under the clay BEST MOM EVER plaque in the garden with Kelsey's tiny handprints embedded in it, she pulled out the spare key to the back door.

Quietly, she crept to the back door, happy that they'd never installed those motion-detection floodlights and security alarm system Aidan constantly talked about. *With a profession like yours,* he'd said, *You just never know what kind of crazies might come around.* They'd been planning on it, and it made sense, but like many things in their lives, they'd put it off.

There was no moonlight at all. Luckily, she'd opened this door enough that she could do it by feel. She twisted the key in the darkness and pushed inside, slowly opening the door so it wouldn't make noise. She pushed it closed behind her, then looked around, inhaling the familiar scent of home.

Tears clouded her vision. She'd missed it so, so much.

She went to the place in the kitchen where they'd eaten their DQ, hours before. It smelled a bit like French fries, but more like the apple cinnamon air freshener she used. The place was a little messier—Mia liked things put away just so, and without her, that had fallen by the wayside—Kelsey's backpack was on the ground, instead of on the hooks near the mudroom. Also, Kelsey's furry, bear-ear hoodie, which she was forever telling her daughter to hang up, was draped over the back of her chair.

Mia lifted it, holding it to her chest, savoring the scent of her daughter's baby shampoo on the hood.

Then, moving on pins and needles, she climbed the steps to the second floor, being careful to avoid the third step, which always creaked awfully.

At the landing, she listened for Aidan's gentle snore. Nothing. She heard him roll over. She wondered if he was sleeping as terribly as she had been. She wanted to go to him, but she couldn't chance that he might wake up.

Instead, she went to her daughter's room. She followed the purple glow of her Rapunzel nightlight and saw Kelsey, lying among her stuffed animals, asleep on her back, both arms stretched above her. She always liked to sleep that way.

Mia sometimes would watch Kelsey from the door of her room as she slept, marveling at how big she'd gotten. But now, her daughter looked practically gigantic, as if she'd aged ten years in these short weeks.

She was still angelic though, still beautiful. It nearly took her breath away.

Kelsey always had been the soundest of sleepers. She didn't even stir when Mia stepped through the threshold into her room, kicking a pair of maracas Kelsey must've left on the floor. Wincing at the sound, she froze, but Kelsey didn't move a muscle.

111

Mia reached down and brushed a lock of blonde hair from her forehead. Taking one of the two burner phones from her pocket, she opened it, making sure it was charged and on, and tucked it under the pillow.

She leaned in to give her a kiss, then decided it was too risky.

"I love you, baby girl," she whispered, and then turned and crept out the way she'd come.

As soon as she was safe in the Honda, she looked at the other phone, desperately wishing she could pick it up and call her daughter, just to hear her speak. She could just imagine her excitement, her fragile, sleepy voice saying, "Mommy?"

But not now. It was too soon. She adjusted her position in the seat, trying to ignore the stabbing pain in her heart, and pointed her car toward the motel.

CHAPTER NINETEEN

The following morning, as the sun crept through the edges of the blackout curtains, Mia looked up at the cottage cheese ceiling, marked with rusting water stains, and rolled over. She'd had less than two hours of sleep.

She picked up the phone and looked at it, wondering if Kelsey had found the phone she'd hid under her pillow, yet. Maybe. But even if she had, she'd be on her way to school, now.

And now, she had other things on her mind. She had to get back to Chloe's place and make sure the police were still on top of it.

She packed up all her things, left the key in the hotel, and loaded everything she owned into her car. She couldn't stay in one place for too long. By now, the Marshals knew she was nearby. They'd be looking for her.

Her only hope was that they wouldn't think she was crazy enough to go back to Chloe's house again.

When she reached the residential neighborhood where the Braxtons had been temporarily relocated, she immediately noticed an official-looking, dark sedan with tinted windows, at the stoplight, heading in the opposite direction. It could've been an undercover police car, so she shrunk down in her seat, hoping the driver didn't notice her.

Slowing as she turned into the development, she looked in her rear-view mirror. The sedan drove off and disappeared onto the main road.

Mia exhaled in relief. Then, she quickly navigated toward Pine Top Trail. The moment she turned onto the road, she slowed to a crawl and looked for the police cars, unmarked or otherwise.

But there were only a few cars there, the same ones she'd noticed up and down the street the day before. A few pick-ups, a couple SUVs. A giant camper, its front on blocks. She inched forward, past the oaks lining the road, until the Braxton home came into view.

It looked quiet. Two cars were parked in the driveway, and that noisy pit bull next door wasn't barking madly. Past the slatted wood fence, toward the back of the house, one of the unicorn pool floats bobbed softly on the surface of the pool.

All was quiet. For a moment, she thought that maybe she'd misunderstood Andrews. Maybe he'd meant something else. But no, that had been him, in the shed, before. Watching the house. She was sure of it.

Or maybe she was just being paranoid, like everyone seemed to think she was.

She noticed an old woman on the other side of the road, walking a teacup poodle and glaring at her suspiciously.

I need to get out of here before the police come after me, she thought.

She was just about to press on the gas when she saw it, on the red Corvette closest to her.

There was what looked like an envelope, made of heavy cream stock, the kind one would use for a wedding invitation, embedded in the frame of the driver's side window. There was some writing on it, in lovely calligraphy.

Maybe it was some formal invitation for a neighborhood party. She inched forward so that she could get a better look and noticed that each one of the cars parked on her side of the residential street had one. There were at least a dozen, all down that side of the tree-lined street. But how odd to leave such a thing on a neighbor's car, instead of in the mailbox.

Her blood ran cold when she was close enough to read the writing on the first envelope.

It said: *Agent Mia North.*

Gasping, she threw her car into park and scrambled out. Grabbing the first one from the Corvette, she rushed to the second, on an SUV. It was the same. *Agent Mia North.*

She plucked that one up, too, and ran to the next. When she'd piled all of them up, she went back to her car and opened the first one, her hands trembling as she lifted out a pretty piece of heavy card stock. On it was more calligraphy. It said:

You're too late, said the spider to the fly. While you wept over the ashes of your old life, I've taken my pound of flesh.

Horror dawned on her as she read the words, once, twice. *The ashes of your old life.*

Had he been following her last night?

And what pound of flesh?

Desperate for answers, she opened the next envelope, and the next. But they all said the same thing.

I've taken my pound of flesh.

I've taken my pound of flesh.

Pound of flesh.

Her heart jumped into her throat as she looked across the street. The day prior, there'd been no cars in the driveway. But now, there were two. They were home. Sleeping in, possibly. Families slept in. That was normal.

She wracked her brain, trying to remember what day it was. Wednesday. Did people sleep in on a Wednesday?

All was quiet, yes. But quiet did not always mean that all was well. Things always fell eerily silent after the worst had happened.

She looped her car around the block and parked on the street there, just in case she needed to make a quick getaway. She pushed open the door, jogged around the block toward Pine Top Trail, and crossed the street to the Braxton house. When she reached the sidewalk, she checked over both shoulders to make sure there were no neighbors or police, watching her. Then she crept along the tree line, toward the house, through grass coated with morning dew.

She stepped around the bushes and landscaping. At the first window, she stood on her tip-toes and peeked in, sneakers digging into the mulch, but the shades were drawn tight.

Skirting the edge of the house, she went to the gate of the chain-link fence, opened it, and slipped inside. At the back corner of the house, she stepped on a river stone edge of the hardscaping around a flower bed and tried to get a peek. But that was closed up, too.

She imagined herself, getting caught, peeking in windows, Mrs. Braxton calling the police on her for being a peeping tom. Her credibility was already shot. If she got caught for this, it would only add to her list of offenses, making her Public Enemy Number One.

But she couldn't help it. Not after those notes she'd received. Wilson Andrews had been here. Stalking them. She had to make sure Chloe was okay. Then she'd make her plans to find this monster, wherever he was, and bring him down, once and for all.

Now, she was in the back of the house. She climbed the stairs to the deck, and the back door. She peered through the glass panes, but saw no movement inside.

Maybe they're all gone, she thought, turning.

She spotted a large bay window, protruding from the back of the house. She'd just begun to take a step over toward it when she caught sight of something horrific.

A smear of fresh blood on the glass.

At first, she could barely register what she was seeing. It was no discernable shape, but there it was, bright and red as if it'd just been shed.

She took a step closer, and that was when she saw something worse, deeper inside the house, on the kitchen's center island.

Chloe's blonde, severed head, resting on the butcher's block, a spray of red shocking against the white cabinetry. Her eyes were closed, her lips bulged, and blood spilled from the severed artery, soaking the top of the counter.

Slumped to its side, on a nearby barstool, was the rest of Chloe, still dressed in a short, blood-soaked nightie and fuzzy slippers.

Mia covered her mouth in horror, but could contain her insides no longer. Turning away from the grisly sight, she rushed over to the bushes and retched, heaving up the meager contents of her stomach.

Chloe . . . dead.

Oh, no, no, no . . . please let this not be true.

As she stood there on her shaking knees, dizzy, trying to stop the world from spinning around her and from losing consciousness, she heard them.

Sirens.

They were coming closer.

But if they wanted to catch the real monster in this case, they, like Mia, were too late.

116

CHAPTER TWENTY

Still reeling, Mia managed to gather her bearings and rush toward the woods at the side of the house, throwing herself over the fence and lying stomach down as the first police car arrived. Once it did, skidding to a stop in the middle of the street outside of the Braxton house, she watched and waited as the two officers exited the vehicle and rushed to the front stoop, anxiously pressing the doorbell and pummeling the door, shouting, "Open up."

As they did, Mia skulked quickly across the street, into some bushes, and made her way through the yards of houses, toward her car. As she slid into the driver's seat and turned the key in the ignition, she thought about what she'd seen. She couldn't get the scene out of her head, and it was likely the police were just stumbling upon it now.

Was there more? Was the entire Braxton family dead in there?

She'd known Wilson Andrews was sick, but she hadn't known just how sadistic he was. Not only had he murdered her, but he'd *decapitated* Chloe.

The vision of her severed head cemented itself in Mia's mind, making her blood run cold as she glanced at the envelopes on the front passenger seat. If he could do something like that . . . what else was he capable of?

She didn't want to know.

She eased away from the curb and slowly pulled around the corner as another police car arrived. When she reached the main road that crossed the entrance to the development, she pounded on the gas and raced out of town, driving blindly, as far and as fast as she could go out of the city.

When she reached Rockwall, she found the nearest liquor store and pulled inside, her head swirling with dark thoughts.

She wasn't much of a drinker—only having a margarita at parties or a glass of wine for dinner— but she bought the first bottle of knock-off Jack she could get her hands on, went to the parking lot, settled in the Honda, and took a swig and closed her eyes, letting the liquid burn its way down her throat.

She hated hard liquor, so she wasn't sure where the impulse had come from. All that went through her head, along with that grisly image of Chloe, was *Numb, numb, numb. Must get numb.*

She'd hoped that would stop her hands from shaking, but they only seemed to get worse as she replayed the scene in her mind. She imagined Chloe, at home, after everything she'd been through, trusting the police to keep her safe . . . only to come face to face with the tormentor they swore they'd protect her from, once again. Mia had thought that part of why Chloe had recovered so quickly was because she barely remembered the torture he'd put her through. Did her memory finally come back to her, in those last moments, when she saw Wilson Andrews's face again?

Mia swallowed the bitter taste in her mouth along with the alcohol. The second swig went down like water, and her vision blurred.

When she regained focus, a woman who exiting the store with a bottle of wine took one look at her and grabbed her child by the hand, ushering her away. Looking around, she realized this place wasn't exactly secluded. There were plenty of shoppers nearby, and her baseball-cap disguise wasn't that foolproof.

She came to her senses and capped the bottle before she went and did something that would add yet another transgression to her growing list of illegalities.

Then she drove her car to an abandoned drive-in movie theater outside of town and parked in the open lot. She stayed there, staring out at the sky and trying to rid herself of that horrific memory.

Was that possible?

At that moment, she didn't think so. Grief and regret overwhelmed her, and she buried her face in her hands.

A man like that, who took life like that, would not ever be redeemed. And yet the more time that went on, the bolder he got.

He probably killed Sara. And he'd kill again.

She needed to stop him. Somehow. Before he destroyed someone else's life.

But how?

The files on him were full of pages and pages of his history. His background ran like a biography of a national hero. On the surface, the man had done no wrong. He'd been an expert in covering his tracks. She had absolutely no clue where he'd strike next.

She scanned to the passenger side of the car, where the bottle of whiskey sat.

Might as well get drunk and pass out here, she thought sourly. At least, out here, she wouldn't have to worry about anyone finding her.

She'd just grabbed ahold of the neck of the bottle when something caught her attention on one of the notecards.

There was a column of dots and dashes at the very bottom of each card, that seemed to bleed over to the next one.

Holding them up, one by one, she confirmed it. It wasn't accidental. Each card had the same, slightly different marking.

She moved the bottle of whiskey to the floor of the car and began to spread the cards out on the seat, matching up the lines and arranging them like a jigsaw puzzle. When she was done, she sat back and read the words that were spread across all twelve cards. It said:

Welcome, said the spider to the fly. You weren't escaping the bus. You were entering my web. We're family now.

She stared at it until the words blurred together. Escaping the bus. Entering his web . . . what on earth was he trying to say to her?

Then she noticed a name, underneath the quote, in smaller script. *Carl Barker and Alice Mays.*

At first, the names didn't sound familiar. Carl and Alice. Alice and Carl. Something about those names, though . . .

At once, she remembered the slovenly guard who'd brought her into the van, and the driver. Yes, Alice was the older driver who'd been less than interested in her partner. Carl had been too interested in his salami sandwich. She'd left them, banged-up but otherwise healthy, when she'd run the van off the road and escaped.

But why would their names be here, on these cards? What was Wilson Andrews trying to say?

An idea came to mind. She grabbed her phone and typed the name in, *Alice Mays,* hoping that her suspicions would not be confirmed . . .

The first search result made the nausea in her throat from earlier that day return:

Texas Corrections Officer Killed by Escaped Convict/Former FBI Agent.

Killed.

She scanned the rest of the article, hardly able to believe what she was seeing: *Alice Mays, a Texas State Corrections Officer, was fatally shot by an escaping prisoner in a prison transfer gone horribly wrong, yesterday afternoon.*

The escaped prisoner, Mia North, is a former FBI agent who was recently convicted of murdering Ellis Horvath. She was being transferred to a maximum-security prison in New Mexico when the incident occurred. According to Carl Barker, another guard who was present during the altercation, the prisoner was able to free herself, wrestle away one of the officers' service revolvers, and use it in the escape. Mays was shot once in the head by the assailant and died at the scene.

Mia reached for the door and manually rolled down the window, trying to drag air into her lungs. But by now, it was later in the day, the sun was hot, and there was no breeze to be found. She couldn't breathe.

She pushed open the door and slid out, onto her hands and knees, gasping as she stared down at the cracked earth.

She'd thought that she'd been alone, on the stretch of land, where she'd crashed that corrections van.

But she hadn't been.

Somehow, Wilson Andrews had been there. He'd had to have been nearby. He shot that officer, and now . . .

Now the police were after her for the murder.

She fell onto her backside and looked up at the sky. She'd escaped to make things right. And now, things were only getting worse.

Wilson Andrews was clearly out to get her. And no one believed her.

He'd taken her freedom. Her livelihood. Everything she loved about her life. What else could he possibly take from her?

The answer struck her right between the eyes, and she let out a muffled whimper.

Grasping for her phone, she called the other burner phone. She'd talk to Kelsey, tell her to put on Aidan, tell them to get away from the house.

But it simply went to a message that said, *This voicemail has not been set up.*

Kelsey probably hadn't found the phone, yet. Mia had always made her daughter make her bed in the morning, but Aidan never insisted on that.

She ended the call and punched in David's number.

Just when she thought it was going to go to voicemail, a groggy voice answered. "Hello?"

"David. It's me. Were you sleeping?"

Now, he sounded wide awake. "I was on nights, last night. Where are you? What's going on?"

"Look. I'm about an hour out of town right now, with traffic . . . I need your help."

"What is it?"

"Wilson Andrews. He killed Chloe Braxton."

"Jesus, Mia. Are you sure? She'd under police surve—"

"I just came from there. She was . . . she was decapitated."

"Holy . . ." A pause. "What were you doing there? Don't you know that if they find you—"

"And he killed---" she swallowed, hardly able to believe it. "You probably saw it on the news. He killed that corrections officer."

"Mia, you understand, they're saying *you* did that?"

"You know I didn't. Please tell me you do."

"Okay, okay. Let me try to understand this. Wilson Andrews, the senate hopeful, followed you out into the desert and killed those guards so that you could escape?"

She winced. When he said it that way, even she didn't believe it. "I know how it sounds."

"And then you just happened to be in the neighborhood to find Chloe's decapitated body?" he asked, his words growing more high-pitched and urgent. "Jesus, Mia."

She gritted her teeth.

"I gave you the benefit of the doubt, Mia, before. Because you were one hell of an agent and I learned a lot from you. I respected you. But now?" He sucked in a breath and let it out. "I don't know what to believe anymore."

"I know. I know that," she said miserably, gripping the phone. She hated to lose his trust, since she'd already lost everyone else's, but she had other things on her mind right now. "I know you've done so much for me. But I need you to do one last thing for me. Please."

He groaned. "You're going to make me lose my job. Worse than that. I can go to *jail*. And then what'll Frank do, without parents to--"

"Please. I've already been through that. But Andrews is insane. He's taken almost everything from me . . . except one thing. I think he's going to go after my family."

A pause. "You want me to call them?"

"I want you to have them put in protective custody. Do whatever you have to do to make it happen. Don't say I'm involved. Just do it. Please."

"Mia . . ."

With that one word, she was certain. He no longer believed her anymore. All of their past history had been erased. He thought he was speaking with a madwoman, a woman who'd kill all those people, based on some sick vengeance plan to make up for the brother she lost, years ago.

"It's Kelsey," she said, her voice small. "I'll never forgive myself if something happens to her. Just think, if it were Frank . . ."

"All right," he said, cutting her off. "I'll do it. What are you going to do?"

"I don't know," she said, ending the call before she could say anything that might give her plans away. Because David was a good man. And though she knew he'd do what he could to keep her family safe, she couldn't trust him not to call the feds on the crazy person who was roaming the streets of Dallas . . . even if it was his own former partner.

*

Traffic headed into Dallas was a bitch.

She wound up stuck on Interstate 30 West, in a dead standstill, which was the normal choke of rush-hour traffic that seemed to plague the city. Rush hour, which ever since Mia could remember, spanned most of the day. Here it was, nearly eight in the evening, and daylight was wasting.

When she pulled into her neighborhood in University Park, the sun had almost completely sunk below the horizon. As she drove onto her street, she prayed, *Please, let David have already removed them to safety.*

But the moment she pulled up to the house, she saw something was wrong. The house was ablaze with lights. They were on in almost every room.

That wasn't like Aidan. How many times had he used that familiar parent-phrase with his daughter? *Kelsey, for the last time, when you leave a room, shut off the lights! What were you, raised in a barn?*

122

Her pulse skittered in her throat as she stepped out of the car and inched closer to the house, her eyes going from window to window.

Eventually, she spied Aidan, in Kelsey's room. He swung his head around, almost frantically, before going to her walk-in closet. He flipped a switch, stepped in, backed out, his mouth contorting into a yell.

Kelsey!

Then he headed into the hall.

In the next moment, he appeared in the master bedroom, once again, his head swinging from side to side. He flipped on the lights in the master bath, then turned and dragged a hand down his face. When he started for the hall again, he was jogging, a look of frustration on his face. He opened his mouth and yelled again.

Kelsey!

Mia let out an uneasy breath as the realization hit her.

Kelsey was gone.

"Oh, my God," she murmured under her breath, breaking into a run.

CHAPTER TWENTY ONE

Frantic, Mia rushed up to the front porch and grabbed the brass door handle, shoving at it. Finding it locked, she pounded with both hands, first open, and then curled into fists.

"Kelsey!" she cried. "Oh, Kelsey, please be all right!"

A moment later, the door opened. Aidan stood there, astonished. "Mimi?" he asked, as if hardly able to believe she was standing there, in front of him. His eyes went wet with tears. "Oh, Mimi!"

He gathered her into his arms and hugged her tight.

"What are you doing here?" he whispered into her ear.

She pulled away and closed the front door behind her. "What happened to Kelsey? Is she here?"

He shook his head. "I don't know. She was here one minute, gone the next. We were packing. We got a call from David, telling us to pack up. So I was getting everything ready, and then she just . . ."

Mia's heart went haywire. She rushed into the living room, looking, with Aidan at her heels, then swept into the rest of the downstairs. "Kelsey!"

Suddenly, the basement door burst open, and Kelsey stood there, holding her princess suitcase. She dropped it immediately when she saw her mother. "Mommy!" she cried, rushing to her.

"Oh, Kelsey!" The girl jumped into her arms, full-force, and Mia squeezed her tight, never wanting to let go. She kissed her cheeks, already finding them wet with tears. "How I've missed you!"

"Mommy. You're not leaving again, are you?" she asked. "Please. You can't."

She blinked hard to keep the tears from flowing. More than anything, she wished she could promise that. But she couldn't. "Where were you?" she asked, smoothing down her hair as she looked at the basement door her daughter had just come from. Kelsey hated the basement. It was dark and scary. She never went down there by herself.

"Daddy said we needed to pack. And I wanted my princess suitcase. I thought it was downstairs, and I was right," she said triumphantly. "Mommy? Are we going on a trip?"

She set Kelsey down and held her hand tight. "I wish I could go with you. But you need to be a big girl and go with Daddy, okay?"

Her lower lip trembled. "But—"

"Please. You need to do as Mommy says."

She nodded, although Mia could tell she was just putting on a brave face. Mia hugged her again. "Okay. Let's get you upstairs so you can finish packing."

They went to the foyer, and Kelsey climbed the stairs up to her room. She was about to follow her up there, but Aidan took her aside and said in a low voice. "Tell me. What's going on?"

"I want to know as well," a voice said behind them.

The two jumped, and Mia instinctively reached for the weapon she didn't have. She let out a breath of relief when she realized it was just David, leaning against the door jamb. He must've let himself in when they'd been running about trying to find Kelsey.

"David," Aidan said with relief, shaking his hand. "Thanks for your call."

They both turned and looked expectantly at Mia.

She took a deep breath, hardly knowing where to start. Then she said, whispering so that her daughter wouldn't overhear, "I know it's hard to believe, but Wilson Andrews is insane. Not only did he kidnap those girls, but he's murdered at least one of them, and two of the guards that were responsible for my prison transfer. He visited me in prison, blamed me for his sinking poll numbers, and now he wants to ruin me, once and for all, so he's pinning all of this on me."

Aidan simply stared. "My God." His eyes filled with sympathy. "Wilson Andrews? Are you sure?"

She nodded.

David stiffened. There was something in his eyes she didn't like. Then he pulled out his phone and said, "Mia, there's something I want to show you. I was going to tell you about it on the phone, but . . ."

He pulled up a video, which he handed to her. On it, Wilson Andrews, dressed in a light gray suit and tie, his thick hair blowing in the breeze, was standing at a podium, doing what he did best, besides getting away with murder—he was making a campaign speech. Her skin crawled as she watched him speak. It looked like he was at a beach resort somewhere, near Galveston. "And?"

"Look at the date."

She did. It had been taped earlier that day, in the morning.

Suddenly, the pieces clicked into place, and she understood.

"How could Wilson Andrews be hundreds of miles away, at the Gulf, and be murdering Chloe Braxton at the same time?" David asked.

"Well . . . I don't know," she murmured, thinking. "He could've done it at night, when—"

"He was at an event in Galveston the night before, and it went late into the night. Do you really think that he'd be able to come all the way back here, then slip back to the hotel, undetected?"

"He could. He has the police in his pock—"

"Come on, Mia. And what about the corrections officers, out near Amarillo? You think he was there, too?"

She stared at him. She had to admit, it was unbelievable. "But I know he did it. I know it. Maybe he hired someone to help him, but . . ."

Aidan took her hand. "Okay, Mimi. I believe you," he said, stroking it gently. "Tell us what evidence you have."

She frowned. She really didn't have anything concrete, except . . .

Reaching into the pocket of her bag, she pulled out the cards that he'd written out to her. She set them out, on the floor, so that her partner and husband could read the message. "He left this for me outside of Chloe's house."

David crouched down, looking at it. "He did?" He picked up the card with the names of the two officers on it. "These are the two corrections officers, huh?"

She nodded.

"Entering his web?" Aidan asked. "This isn't good. We've got to get you out of here, Mimi."

She held up a hand. "No, you've got to get out of here." She looked at David hopefully.

David nodded. "Right. I've got a place I can take your family to, until all of this gets figured out. We ready?"

Aidan shook his head, but just then, Kelsey appeared at the top of the staircase. "Ready. Hi, Agent Hunter."

"Hi, sweetheart," he said to her. "We're going on a little trip."

They went outside, and after tearful goodbyes, David loaded them into his SUV.

"Where are you going to take them?" she asked.

"You know the place. North. All right?"

126

She nodded. There was only one safe house up north, about a hundred miles from the city, in a secluded section of Lake Kiowa. It was so secret, very few people on the force even knew about it. The only reason David knew was because she'd told him.

Yes, it was the best place for her family, right now.

He looked at Mia. "What are you going to do now?"

She shrugged. She still wasn't sure whether he believed her or not. The evidence wasn't very convincing—she could've created those cards herself. "I don't know. None of this makes sense. I need to go somewhere and think."

"All right," he said, reaching out to shake her hand. "Good luck."

"Thanks, David," she said. She watched them pull out of the driveway, waving and blowing kisses to Kelsey until they disappeared from sight.

*

An hour later, Mia found herself in a corner booth at a little hole-in-the-wall coffee shop, far away from the bustle of the city, staring at a news story on her phone:

Mentally Ill Escaped Convict Allegedly Murders Kidnapping Victim

Mia gulped her coffee. Mentally Ill?

And now, they were pinning Chloe's murder on her, too, saying she was responsible for a string of felonies stretching all across Northern Texas.

It was more than a total stretch—it was unbelievable. The investigating officer in charge of Chloe's murder, some Detective Winegrass at the Dallas PD, had made the case that Mia was frustrated at Chloe's amnesia, and her inability to point a finger at Wilson Andrews as her kidnapper. *Reports indicate that Mia North may be suffering from psychological trauma stemming from past events, which may have contributed to her decision to stalk the suspects in the cases she was involved in, including state senate hopeful Wilson Andrews and science teacher Ellis Horvath, who she was convicted of murdering earlier this month.*

They'd even found fresh evidence that Mia had been at Chloe's house recently, which bolstered their case.

She desperately wanted to throw her phone against the wall.

It was well after the dinner rush, if a greasy spoon like that even had a rush, so she was the only customer. The waitress there, a haggard older woman who seemed as if she was half-asleep herself, didn't bother her after handing over her salad, except to come by and fill her coffee mug whenever it got empty.

There, she spread out all of her files about the case and huddled over all of it, wearing a flannel David had provided, collar pulled up to hide her face. Both cook and waitress seemed focused on the television above the counter, where some all-important baseball game droned on. Every once in a while, a bat would crack and one of them would shout out in glee or frustration.

Other than that, it was a nice, peaceful break from the past few days.

She looked over the contents of the folder—witness statements, crime scene reports from that place on Prescott, police interviews of Wilson Andrews—trying to see if there was anything else she'd missed.

Rubbing her bleary eyes, she sighed. She'd looked over all of this, a thousand times. What, exactly, was she thinking she'd find, now?

She knew it was Wilson Andrews. It had to be. So what if he'd been in Galveston? Maybe he'd found a way to evade his people and get back to Dallas to commit the crime. Maybe the time of Chloe's death had been earlier, before he left for Galveston. Or maybe . . .

Maybe he'd had an accomplice.

That seemed much more reasonable. But who? He had so many associates, literally hundreds of people in his circle who could've helped him out.

Mia turned a paper and scanned some more, then yawned.

Her eyes fell on the notecards he'd sent her. She pulled them close to her and assembled them, once again, so that they made the message:

Welcome, said the spider to the fly. You weren't escaping the bus. You were entering my web. We're family now.

I wasn't escaping the bus. I was entering his web, she thought to herself.

Yes, Wilson Andrews's web. He certainly had one of those, with all these interconnecting strands, a network so big and complicated that she had no idea how to get out of it, now. He had not only the mental acuity, but the resources to set her up. He could easily fudge evidence and influence the police so that they believed every last lie he fed them.

Wilson Andrews had visited her, shortly before anyone knew she was about to be transferred. But he'd known, probably from his connections. But which connections had he used? Someone on the inside, close to the prison system.

And why had he come to her? Simply to get the last laugh?

Or was it much more sinister than that?

He knew her. He knew what lengths she'd go to, in order to protect someone. He knew that given the chance . . . she would try to escape and save Chloe.

Suddenly, it came to her. The too-loose shackles on her wrist. The fat, slovenly guard who seemed to put up hardly any resistance at all.

Had Wilson Andrews orchestrated this whole thing, making her jailbreak possible?

For what reason? So he could continue killing these people who'd wronged him, who maybe knew something about Sara Waverly, and have someone to blame for it? So that the world would never find out what horrible things he had done?

Mia tapped the side of the table, thinking. If it was that, then who would be next?

She didn't know, but finally, she had an idea of who might.

Draining the last of her coffee, she piled up her things, gathered them under her arm, left a twenty-dollar bill to take care of the check, and headed outside.

CHAPTER TWENTY TWO

Mia knew this was dangerous.

Going back to the Dallas prison where she'd been incarcerated felt like crawling into the belly of the beast.

But she had no choice.

She looked up at the monstrous, nondescript brick building with its miniscule windows, the back half surrounded by a two-story-high brick wall. Even now, the place made her shiver. For a moment, she thought of Shilah, and Angel Vasquez, and all the other people she'd met behind bars. She wondered if they were following her case, since the transfer.

Oh, who was she kidding? *Everyone* was following the case of the FBI agent who'd gone off the deep end and was now murdering people across the state. She was the top story in every news outlet in the Southwest.

Which meant she had to be all the more careful. She couldn't chance being seen in public anymore. Everyone was on the lookout for her, now. Her window of time to apprehend Chloe's killer was quickly closing.

That was why she shivered as she sat there, even in that empty, unlit back corner of the parking lot, practically hidden among the encroaching weeds.

She had to be careful with her time. She couldn't afford to make any mistakes right now.

She knew the schedules of most of the prison guards, from the weeks she'd spent there. There was very little to do, other than staring at a blank wall, so she'd observed their comings and goings, listened to their conversations, learned things about the way the prison worked.

So she knew that, as luck would have it, Carl Barker, when he wasn't engaged in a prison transfer, had a shift that ended at ten PM, right after lights out.

She waited at the fence by the employee lot, for him to go through security and step outside. She saw him get into his old, dented Chevy Malibu with the broken taillight, and speed off, toward town. She followed him, keeping a safe distance as he stopped into a McDonald's drive through for a happy meal. One happy meal. That meant he lived alone.

Good.

She continued pursuing him until he pulled into a two-story apartment complex a few miles away, at Oak Lawn.

The parking lot was gated, so she pulled to the side of the road as he parked. He took his time, lumbering toward the complex, sipping his extra-huge Coke and munching on fries from the bag as he walked.

She waited in the bushes, watching as he stopped at the first apartment in the narrow alleyway. When he twisted the key, she came up behind him, pulled out his gun, and placed it squarely between his fleshy shoulders.

"Remember me?" she said, nudging him through the door.

He dropped his Coke. "Dammit! Dude! You scared the life out of me! And you--"

"Move!" she snarled, digging the barrel of the gun into his back. "And shut up."

He staggered forward, and when they were both through, she slammed the door and pulled off the trucker's hat, shaking out her hair. He looked over his shoulder and let out a groan.

"Oh, no. Not again."

She smiled as she pushed him farther into the apartment, hitting a wall of nauseating, competing smells—garbage, the syrup of this morning's breakfast, and body odor, mingling with the too-thick spice of cheap cologne . . . or was that old barbecue sauce? It was hard to tell. She swallowed back the urge to retch and whispered, "Nice to see you, too, Carl."

He held up his hands and danced back and forth in the foyer, his pants sagging even more dangerously, close to slipping. When he turned, she noticed a bandage on his forehead. "What do you want from me?"

"I think you know," she said, motioning with the gun for him to sit at the kitchen table. It was covered with dirty dishes and crumpled fast food bags. He sat down on one end, and she sat down at the other, grimacing at a bowl full of sour milk and soggy O's. When she pushed it away, several fruit flies scattered. She groaned. "God, Carl, you're a slob. Anyone ever tell you that?"

He looked like he was about to cry. She wasn't sure if it was because of the gun, or because he'd spilled his soda. He reached into the bag and pulled out a fry. "I don't know. I didn't do nothin' wrong."

"Don't give me that. I knew it was too easy, how I escaped," she said, glancing around the room. The rest of the place wasn't much better. It was like an episode of *Hoarders,* full of so much trash, she couldn't see the real apartment underneath. "Any guard worth his salt would never loosen the restraints the way you did."

He stared for a beat, then looked into the fast-food bag and pulled out his sandwich. He carefully unwrapped it, licking his fat lips. "I have no idea what you're talking about."

She reached over and picked up the sandwich, sending lettuce flying. He tried to snatch it back, but she stuck the gun in his nose. "Focus, Carl."

He sighed, still eyeing the sandwich. "On what?"

She wanted to toss the Bic Mac in the trash, but she knew he'd only complain. So she said, "Tell me. Did someone pay you to make it easy for me to escape?"

"Pay me?"

She snapped her fingers. "You know what I'm getting at. Talk." She looked at the Big Mac, gauging what would hurt him most. A bullet in the head, or a lost sandwich? "Or I eat your Big Mac."

Not that she would, but it had the result that she wanted. He said, "Don't. Fine. Yeah. Someone paid me. Not a lot. Only a thousand. If I knew what a pain in the ass you'd be, I'd have asked for double."

So she'd been right. "What was his name?"

He shrugged. "Don't know."

She kicked him under the table. "Come on."

"Ow! I seriously don't know."

"Was it Wilson Andrews?"

He let out an incredulous laugh. "Right. I've been reading about you. And your obsession with that politician. You ain't gonna let that go, are you? They're gonna hang you, and you're still going to be spouting off about what a criminal he is. Aren't you?"

She scowled. "Was it?"

"*No,*" he said with a great deal of satisfaction. "It wasn't."

She stared at him, waiting for more.

Finally, he cracked. "Look, I don't know who he is. We met twice at the Blue Moon Diner, on the corner of Oak Lawn and Tenth. He never stayed for longer than five minutes, and he wore a baseball cap and sunglasses and a shaggy beard that I'm pretty sure was a disguise. So I couldn't point him out if he walked right in this room and did a jig on this table."

"And he paid you a thousand dollars? What else?"

"What do you mean, what else? I was eating breakfast there one day, and he showed up and said he knew who I was and asked if I wanted to make a quick thou. I said I was interested. He took down my number and told me he'd call with more details. A week later, he called and I met him at the diner. That's where he gave me the cash and told me that all I needed to do was loosen the restraints so you could get out, and he'd do the rest. That's all."

"That's all?"

He nodded. "Well. He told me that no matter what I saw when I was out there, the only thing I could tell the police was that you overpowered me and escaped."

"What about Alice. What happened to Alice?"

His eyes narrowed to slits. "You should know. You shot her."

"But you didn't see that."

He snorted. "How could I? I was unconscious."

"And when you came to? Was there anyone at the scene that maybe shouldn't have been?"

He shook his head. "I only woke up when I was in the hospital. Thanks to you. You did a number on me." He pointed to the bandage on his forehead. "Concussion. I was in the hospital for two days. I just got back to work this morning."

Poor baby, she thought with no sympathy whatsoever. "All right." She stood up and placed the sandwich on the silver wrapper.

He pounced on it like a hungry lion, tearing a giant bite. "Hey," he said, mouth full. "You're not going to tell anyone that I did that thing? With the restraints? I don't want to lose my job?"

"That depends," she said, holding up the gun. "Are you going to tell the police that I visited you?"

He shook his head. "I promise."

"And one other thing. Your next answer is your stay-out-of-jail card. You didn't happen to see what kind of car the man at the diner drove?"

He nodded and swallowed. "How couldn't I see it? It was one of those tow trucks. But not a small one, for cars. One for towing big rigs."

Mia nodded. "Good. Did you see a name on it?"

"I did, but . . . damned if I can remember it. Something with a J or an R. Local. It said it was from Dallas. A name, I think. But that's all I got."

She headed for the door, navigating around the garbage and shaking her head. As she reached the door, he called, "Please don't take my gun. They already gave me shit about when you grabbed the other one from me."

"Fine." She set it down on a flowered couch that was covered in crates of garbage. "And Carl? Clean this place up."

CHAPTER TWENTY THREE

As the night went on, Mia drove aimlessly around the industrial section of Dallas, looking for any sign of a tow service that handled the bigger rigs. She found one, Annie's. It was a name, at least, even if it didn't have a J or R in it. But when she went to the windows and looked inside, she saw an AVAILABLE sign in the door. It appeared to not be in business anymore.

Getting back into her car, she drove up and down another mostly empty street. As she meandered about, driving around the semis parked at the sides of the road, she scrolled through the listings on her burner phone.

Skip's Towing Service

AAA Towing

The Best Towing Service

Nothing that seemed remotely close to what Carl had described.

But maybe he was just giving her bogus information so she would get lost? And she'd assumed the place had to be somewhere among the factories and warehouses, because it just made sense, but maybe that hunch was wrong. Maybe this was a wild goose chase.

Just as she was about to give up, she scrolled to a business called Jiffy Jerry's Towing and Automotive.

The listing said that it was open twenty-four hours, so she placed a call. "Jiffy Jerry's!" a pleasant male voice said. "This is Bruce. How can I help you?"

"Hi, um . . ." she started, not really knowing where she was headed. She really should've planned this a little better, before placing the call. "I am a graduate student, doing a report on different businesses. I found yours and was wondering if you could tell me a little bit about your business."

"Uh, sure, why not?" the man said. "What can I do you for? Where do you go?"

"Oh. University of Dallas," she said automatically, trying to keep herself calm. "So, where are you located?"

"On International Drive, by the business park and the old train station."

Mia looked around. She knew where that was. It was less than a mile away, past the highway.

"And you're the owner?"

"Oh, no. Not me. My cousin Jerry owns the place. He's been in the business for twenty years."

"So, you tow big rigs, huh?"

He chuckled. "Yeah, we do that, and we rent out other vehicles to people as well. We only got one big rig tower that we use to tow semis around the area to the garage, but my cousin has a fleet of over three-hundred other vehicles he rents out. He's a pretty big name in the industry, for sure. You need a vehicle, come to Jiffy Jerry's!"

What a great advertisement for his cousin's business, this Bruce guy was. "Three-hundred! And how do you keep track of all of those cars?"

More laughter. "Well, it's easy, with GPS. I do it myself. I can tell you where any one of our fleet of cars and trucks has been at any time of the day, no matter when it is, with my computer."

"Oh, really!" she gushed. "That's really cool. Would you be able to show me that? I'm in the neighborhood. And I've always been really interested in the technical stuff."

"Sure. Hop on over. I'll be here all night. We're a twenty-four-hour business. You can keep me company."

She suppressed a groan. She really hoped he wouldn't be the kind that would try to flirt with her. She really didn't need that right now. "Okay! I'm on my way!"

She pressed on the gas as she ended the call. She turned a corner and saw a truck, parked on the edge of a rutted field of mud and refuse. Her headlights illuminated the Jiffy Jerry's Automotive Service sign painted on its door. Beyond it was a one-story white building, its windows ablaze in light. Inside, she could see all the markings of a regular office—a front counter for customers, and employee desks beyond.

She parked in one of the customer parking spots and went inside, looking around. The sparkling white waiting area was vast and clean, and everything looked new, the magazines on the coffee table arranged with almost military precision. There was a water cooler and coffee service in the corner, and a tray of packaged pastries waiting nearby, along with a sign that said, *Make yourself at home while you wait*! Jerry had done quite well for himself. But there was no one there.

She picked up a business card on the counter and resisted ringing the service bell. She'd just been on the phone with him. Probably just went to the restroom. He'd return soon.

After a minute, she began to get impatient. Drumming her fingers on the counter, she called, "Bruce?" Then she leaned in and looked at the computer behind the counter. It seemed to be running a fairly simple GPS program, similar to the one she'd seen used in the FBI, to track their agents' vehicles.

Hmm. She reached over and tested the swinging half-door to the back area. It wasn't locked. She could probably just zip in there and get the info she needed, herself.

Before she'd even thought it fully through, she'd pushed through and nudged aside the office chair. She scanned the picture list of vehicles and found the only truck that was large enough to be the big rig Carl had seen outside the diner when he'd met with the man who'd bribed him to loosen her restraints. She found it, then navigated back to the address of the Blue Moon diner.

Several of Jiffy Jerry's vehicles had been there over the past three months, but the rig had been there, twice. The second time was the day before Mia's scheduled transfer.

Bingo.

Quickly, she grabbed another piece of paper and wrote the license plate of the rig. If only Bruce would come back, she could ask if he knew who had been driving it. She looked around, wondering where they kept that information on file, and noticed something.

A small, black wet drop, on the edge of the dark laminate counter.

She looked closer. Because the desk was black, it was hard to tell what it was. She touched it, and the pad of her finger came back red.

Blood.

Alarmed, now, she moved away from the desk, trying to keep calm. *Bruce just had a bloody nose, that's all,* she told herself. *Everything is fine.*

Then she saw the much larger puddle of blood, gathered around her feet.

*

Mia rushed outside, breathing hard, the metallic scent of blood thick in her nostrils.

She knew she was leaving her fingerprints and DNA all over that crime scene, but by now, did it matter? She was already due to have the book thrown at her. All she could think about was getting as far away from the grisly sight as possible.

Outside, though, she doubled over, swallowing again and again to keep from retching. The world spun circles around her as she braced her hands on her thighs, half-formed thoughts trailing through her mind.

Wilson Andrews, or whoever was doing this, was one step ahead of her. He knew she'd be coming after him.

He seemed to know everything she was thinking, as if he was right inside her mind.

Heart pounding, she went to her car. She was just about to open the driver's side door of the hatchback when she noticed the trail of blood.

It wasn't much of a trail, just two or three drops, at random intervals, heading across the parking lot. Why hadn't she noticed it before? She followed it with her eyes, until it stopped right at the door to the rig.

When she stepped closer, she saw a form sitting in the truck. At first, she thought it was only the seat back, but then she realized it was a person, wearing a plaid shirt, arm casually hooked out the window.

The only problem was that there were droplets of blood, dripping from the limp, extended hand.

Moving closer, already biting her tongue for fear of what she might find, she took out the cell phone and turned on the flashlight, arcing it over the scene.

The man, Bruce, possibly, was sitting in the driver's seat of the cab. But it would be impossible to tell who it was, even if she had known the man, because the head was completely gone. He'd been decapitated, too.

She brought her closed fist to her mouth to keep from letting out a cry.

Then, she looked around. She was alone here.

But now she knew better. She was *never* alone, anymore.

He was watching her. Somehow. Getting ready to play his next trick.

Mia was jolted from her horror by the sound of canned television sit-com laughter coming from somewhere up above. She looked around and realized there was an open window on the second floor. It looked like there was an apartment up there. Though the lights were off, she could see the white-blue glow of a television set, shadows moving around it.

Scanning the building, she saw a set of metal stairs, leading up to the landing. She could feel her pulse, pounding in her neck. Something about that room seemed to beckon to her, telling her that she would find the answers there.

She took a step toward her car, but stopped. If she got in her car, where would she go, then? She'd be at a dead end. And the killings would only continue.

No. She needed to do this.

Clenching her hands into fists, she slowly stepped up the staircase, her feet making a pinging sound, no matter how quiet she tried to be. Now, she could not only hear her pulse, but her thudding heart, along with the canned laughter from that stupid sitcom. She recognized some of the voices. It sounded like *Diff'rent Strokes.* She could've sworn she heard Arnold say, "What you talkin' 'bout, Willis?"

Sure enough, at the top of the landing, the door was slightly ajar. Welcoming her.

She pushed it open, wishing she'd had Carl's gun. Now, she was defenseless.

The first thing she spotted, on the ground, was a pile of old hubcaps. Then, a few dusty milk crates that appeared to be full of auto parts. The floor was wood-slatted, covered in grime. The smell was of motor oil and mold.

It looked like a place for storage, only. Not an apartment. Maybe it had once been one, though. There was a fireplace along the wall, and there were even a few framed photographs on the mantle.

She didn't want to venture in. It was a trap. Something in the back of her mind told her that. So, keeping her feet firmly planted in the threshold of the door, she reached over and lifted one of the pictures into her hands.

But as she lowered her head to stare at the photograph of two men, she pushed the door open a little more, and saw more things that did not belong in a storage room. Deeper in the room, a little corner had been set up as a living area, with an oval area rug and floor lamp. An overstuffed, plaid couch, kind of like the one Mia's grandmother had decades ago. It was facing away, toward a console television, the massive, walnut kind that weighed as much as a car but had a tiny screen in proportion. Sure enough, Arnold was on, in black and white, saying something cheeky to Mrs. Garrett. More canned laughter ensued.

Mia focused in on the head, sticking up above the back of the couch. It was set there, absolutely still.

She hoped it was still attached to a body. She'd seen enough bodies without heads to last a lifetime.

She wanted to stay outside. But she couldn't help it. She took a step. Then another. As she moved closer, she saw the long, blonde hair, and gasped. She knew that hair.

Sara Waverly.

She took another step forward. She thought about the pictures of the girl in the folder. Sara Waverly, so full of life. So happy and young, with her entire future ahead of her. This man, this monster, had come and destroyed her. For a moment, she wished she could turn back time.

"Sara?" she whispered.

No response. The absolute stillness was heartbreaking. Mia knew something was wrong. *Please don't be dead.*

She came close enough to touch, and put a hand on the girl's shoulder. She didn't feel a living thing beneath her fingers, though. It was hard. Like a block of ice.

She moved slightly around the girl and saw the smiling, slightly wooden expression of a mannequin, gazing blankly into the distance. Drawn, pale cheeks, exaggeratedly long neck, and now that she looked at it, fake nylon hair that was nothing like Sara's. The mannequin was naked, except for a note, pinned to its chest, in that same, pretty calligraphy:

Told you we're family. See you soon at the reunion.

She looked down at the photograph in her hands. It was a picture of two men, at a graduation, somewhere. The man in the cap and gown looked familiar.

Very familiar.

But the other man . . . who was he?

Oh, no.

Her heart dropped to her stomach, and now, she knew exactly where to go.

140

She could only hope that she wasn't too late.

CHAPTER TWENTY FOUR

Mia drove frantically, hardly paying attention to the street signs.

It had begun to drizzle as she left Jiffy Jerry's, but now, the rain was coming down in buckets, fogging the windshield and making it hard to see. She fumbled to find the defrost as she careened into darkness, not sure exactly where she was headed.

She'd only been to the house on Lake Kiowa once, at the beginning of her career, for a training exercise. It was a rustic cabin, very no-nonsense, with minimal furniture, like a rental cabin. It was always stocked with the necessities for an emergency stay, but it wasn't exactly homey. The one plus? It was right on a bluff, overlooking the pristine lake.

Mia only hoped she remembered how to get to that bluff. She recalled an old ma-and-pa convenience store-slash-gas station named Mort's, and a narrow trail that was almost impossible to see among the pines . . . but she had no choice.

She had to get there. Somehow.

Told you we're family. See you soon at the reunion.

Family. Yes, the safe house was supposed to be concealed. But after everything this killer had known about her, after all the ruthless, daring things he'd done, she knew not to underestimate him.

This killer. Whoever he was.

She looked at the photograph on the passenger seat. It clearly depicted Wilson Andrews, years ago, at his graduation. He had some connection with Jiffy Jerry's, and it pained her to think just what it was.

That was why he could be everywhere at once. He'd had an accomplice, Jiffy Jerry.

According to her estimations, the safe house was still an hour away. She thought of Kelsey, there, probably tossing and turning in a bed that wasn't hers. Of Aidan, sitting up with a book, unable to sleep because he was sick with worry.

And she thought of this killer . . . lurking outside.

She grasped at her chest and pounded the accelerator with her foot.

As she pulled off the interstate to take the highway that led up to the lake, she skidded to a stop at the sight of dozens of red taillights, lined up, stretching into the distance.

Far away, the lights of a police car flashed blue and red against the slick surfaces of the rocks hugging the curve of the road.

Great. Perfect, she thought, typing the address of the safe house into her GPS for alternate directions to the house on Lake Kiowa. Not that it mattered. She was stuck on the ramp, surrounded by cars. She couldn't get out, even if she wanted to.

She banged the heel of her hand on the steering wheel and looked around in frustration.

She'd just begun to take her burner phone out of her pocket when the cars ahead of her began to move again. The rain was pounding the roof of her car like a thousand little drummers. She inched through the weather, hugging tight to the bumper of the car in front of her.

As she moved off the ramp, she realized most of the cars were doing a U and heading the opposite way on the highway, their headlights momentarily blinding her as they drove past.

That was when she saw the police officer in the dark black slicker, waving people on. The cars in front of her powered down their windows, and he spoke to them briefly, pointing.

Even better, she thought, grabbing her hat and tucking her hair underneath it.

When she came to him, she rolled down the window and said, keeping her head mostly in the shadows, "Can't I go through that way?"

"Nope, ma'am. Bridge is out. There's a detour if you go west for about five miles and take the old logging road, but it's gonna set you back thirty min—"

She pressed on the gas, swerving into the gravel of the median before taking off on the road. Thirty minutes. She couldn't wait that long. For all she knew, the killer was already there.

Thrusting a hand in her pocket for her phone, her fingers sliced a small rectangle of card stock. She grimaced, pulling her hand out, sucking on the tip of her finger, tasting blood from the papercut. Papercuts, no matter how small they were, always stung the worst.

Then she remembered what it was—the business card from Jiffy Jerry's.

143

She pulled it out of her pocket, popped the overhead interior light on, and for the first time, *really* looked at it.

She nearly swerved off the road as her worst suspicions were confirmed.

Jiffy Jerry's Automotive Service
Sales and Rentals
Jerry Andrews, Owner

Andrews. Jerry Andrews was Wilson Andrews's family. From the photograph she'd seen, and the similarity in the faces, she gauged they were brothers.

Of course. The Andrews family was big and powerful. They took care of their own. And there were no lengths a public figure like him wouldn't go to in order to protect his family secrets. Wilson Andrews had been doing all of this, framing her, not to protect himself, but to protect his wayward brother.

And now they were due for a reunion.

Driving treacherous speeds along the slick, unfamiliar roads, she only slowed to punch in Aidan's number. She listened as the phone rang, and rang, and rang, before finally going to voicemail.

She hit redial, clutching the phone in her sweat-dampened hand. Same result.

"Dammit, Aidan, pick up!" she barked into the phone.

Then she remembered the burner phone she'd given to her daughter. She'd put the number into her phone, but when she'd seen Kelsey, she hadn't asked her if she'd found it. She dialed that number, but the ringing only made her stomach sink more. No answer.

Besides, Kelsey was probably sleeping. The best she could do was send a text and hope she woke and saw it. With one hand, she typed in:

It's mom. Get out of the safe house. I will be there soon. Xo.

Then she pressed "send" and hoped for the best.

CHAPTER TWENTY FIVE

Kelsey rolled over in her strange new bed.

She didn't understand why her mom was gone. Was it something she'd done? Her father said it wasn't, that her mom just needed to go away. Billy Sheridan said she'd been thrown in the slammer for some pretty bad things. He'd said she went to the court, and the court found her guilty, and that she'd "rot" in jail for the rest of her life.

But if that was true, why had she visited them today? What was going on?

She stared at the ceiling. There was a light outside, shining through the window into the small bedroom, illuminating the rivulets of falling rain on the panes. Here, the rain sounded so loud, like an army, marching across the roof. The place smelled funny, like old people. The room was too cold. And it was really muddy outside, so muddy, she'd ruined her new sneakers. She didn't understand why she had to be here, in the middle of the night, in this terrible place.

And most of all, she didn't understand why her mom couldn't come with her. Was she in trouble? Had she done bad things?

No. Not her mom. Her mom made her grilled cheese and tomato soup every time she asked for it. Her mom read her favorite book to her, *The Princess Plan,* about a thousand times, before she could read it herself. Her mom always treated everyone well. She didn't even yell at the man who'd hit the bumper of their car at the supermarket parking lot, that time.

It didn't make any sense.

Bad things? *What* bad things, exactly? Her mom was an FBI agent. And when she'd asked her dad what that meant, he'd said, *She catches the bad guys.*

Catches the bad guys. She wasn't a bad guy, herself. That was impossible. She was sure of it.

She rolled over in bed and pulled the sheet up to her chin, trying to get warm. Every time she asked Dad, though, he told her not to worry. How could she believe that, when he was obviously so worried himself?

He *always* tried to shield her from things. They no longer watched the news during dinnertime. Whenever anyone came to visit and asked about Mom, he always spoke in hushed tones, so she couldn't hear.

So it was probably bad. Dangerous.

That was why they were all the way out here, in the middle of nowhere, right? That was why two guards with guns had met them when they pulled down this long, muddy driveway. That was why David and her dad had barely spoke, the whole hour-long drive, and whenever they did, it was like they were talking in code, leaving important parts of the conversation out. As they did, they kept glancing into the back seat at her, exchanging worried glances. She probably could've cut the tension in the car with a knife.

And another thing. David had gone back to work, and had left them with a couple of other agents Kelsey had never seen before. He'd told them they'd be safe and snug here. Now, Dad was in the living room, reading some book he'd found. Every so often, she could hear him turn the page and let out a little sigh. When she'd asked him if he was going to bed, he'd said he wasn't tired. It was probably after midnight.

He wasn't fooling anyone. She may have only been eight, but she knew it better than anyone. Something was wrong.

Kelsey was getting a sniffle. She needed a tissue. Slipping out of bed to go in search for one, she glanced at the phone near her pillow.

It was lit up.

Funny. She'd always been telling her parents that she wanted a real-looking play phone, not one of those goofy, bright-colored ones with the giant buttons, that played "Twinkle Twinkle Little Star" whenever she turned it on. She kept telling them it would be great "practice" for the real phone they'd promised to get her when she turned twelve.

They'd had an argument, the night before, because at the basketball game, Kelsey had been acting out. Pushing other kids. She'd just had a bad day because she'd failed a math test, since her mom was always the one to sit with her and help her understand things. Fractions were terrible—she couldn't figure them out. It was so frustrating, not having a mom around, and not having anyone to talk to her straight, and tell her what was going on.

After he'd yelled at her on the court, Dad had apologized for losing his cool. He'd seemed really sad that he'd lost it on her, like that.

So she thought he'd gotten her that phone, as a peace offering. He hadn't outright given it to her—he'd left it under her pillow. She'd spent a little time downloading games on it, playing Fruit Ninja and Minecraft, but that was all. Then she'd put it on Do Not Disturb—she always saw her mom doing that—so she wouldn't get any notifications from the games at night.

But now, weirdly . . . it was glowing, the display all lit up, so bright it illuminated the whole bedroom.

She lifted the phone and looked at it.

There was a single message there. It said: *It's mom. Get out of the safe house. I will be there soon. Xo.*

Mom? She stared at it, confused. Why was her mom texting her on a play phone? She didn't even know the phone had texting capabilities. This was weird.

She wondered for a moment if she should text back. But for the past few weeks, she felt like everything she did was wrong. Messing up in basketball. Talking to Billy Sheridan. Failing math. Asking questions about mom that he refused to answer. Dad was so angry at her, now. She didn't want to do the wrong thing again.

The stone floor was ice-cold, so cold, it stung her bare feet. She padded to the door and pushed it open. Warm orange light flooded her eyes, making her blink as she walked into the tiny living area with the big stone fireplace. "Dad?"

He looked up and sighed. "I thought you'd gone to bed."

"But . . ." She brought the phone over to him and laid it on the wooden armrest. "I think I got a text from mom on my play phone."

His face went from annoyance to confusion in a blink. "Play phone?" He stared at it, then picked it up. "Wait. Where did you get this?"

For a second, she was pretty sure she'd done something wrong again, so she stammered. "D-didn't you leave it in my bedroom? Under my pillow?"

"When?"

"I—I found it. Yesterday. In the morning. I thought you—"

He rose to his feet, still staring at the text, and raked a hand through his hair. "What the—"

"Is everything okay, Dad? Should we get out of here, like the message says?"

He shook his head slightly, his lips moving as he reread the message on the phone. "I don't know." Then he headed for the door.

"Let me talk to the guards and see what's going on. I'll be right back. Stay here."

Without waiting for her to respond, he opened the front door and went outside. She scurried over to the front window and stood on her toes to peer out.

There, she saw her father, showing the phone to the two burly men outside. They'd been rooted in the same spot for hours, on either side of the door. Now, the three men looked at the message, and she could see their faces, wrinkled in confusion, in the dim blue glow of the phone.

No one knew what was going on.

But now, Kelsey had a pretty good idea about one thing: That play phone probably *wasn't* a play phone.

Had her mom left it for her?

Funny, a couple nights ago, during the few hours when she was actually able to sleep, she'd had a dream about that. Her mom had come in, touched her head, and said, *Love you, baby girl.* But that had just been a dream. Hadn't it?

She heard her father say, "Well, what should we do about it? Do you think we should go somewhere?"

One of the guards said, "No. Where would we take you? This place is secure. No place more secure than this."

Her father looked doubtful. "Yeah, but . . . if my wife is trying to get here . . . it must mean that we're in danger."

"If she's trying to get here, we're going to put handcuffs on her and get her to authorities. She's a wanted woman, Mr. North."

He shook his head. "Something's wrong. Are you sure—"

"Look, Mr. North. Go inside. We've got this under control," the other guard said, cutting him off.

Kelsey didn't like that guard talking to her dad that way. He hesitated there, then retreated to the cabin.

Kelsey pushed away from the window and tried to pretend like she hadn't been eavesdropping in on the adult conversations. Her father hated when she did that. She fidgeted from foot to foot on the icy floor as he stepped inside and shook the raindrops from his hair. When he closed the door, he stood there, staring at the message.

"Dad?"

He was so deep in thought that he looked up, a little startled, as if he hadn't expected to be there. "Hmm?"

"Is everything all right?"

"I don't know . . ." he said, and then his tone changed. "Hey. I got an idea."

"What?" she asked, suspicious. She got suspicious whenever he put on that overly happy tone. The first time he'd done it, she'd been three, and he'd been trying to get her to eat broccoli—"Try this, you'll love it!"—and he'd used it many times since. She didn't trust it.

"Get your shoes on, and your blanket and pillow. I saw an old milk house out back. Let's check it out."

"Milk house?"

"Yeah, come on," he said, nudging her toward the bedroom. "Come on. Let's get a move on."

There was a little more urgency in his voice now. Now, she really didn't trust him. Like it was a normal thing to head out in the rain, in the dark of night, to check out some dusty old outbuilding? *Not.*

"Oooookay," she said, rolling her eyes. *My dad's gone totally off his rocker,* she said to herself, but even then, she'd begun to get worried. This wasn't about getting her to eat some vegetables she hated. This was serious.

She did as he asked her to, going back to her room, scuffing into her already-muddy sneakers, and grabbing her blanket and unicorn stuffie. Since she was cold, she put on her hoodie, too, then went out to find her father, pacing the floor.

Without a word, he lunged forward and took her hand, ushering her through a small mudroom, to the side door of the house. When he opened it, she saw the crumbling white plaster of a tiny building that was no bigger than a shed. It had no windows, only a wooden door that seemed to be hanging at an angle.

As she looked at the place, blinking the rain from her eyes, there was only one word that came to mind: Spiders.

Lots and lots of spiders.

There was a path between the two buildings, but it was covered in muddy ruts.

She looked back at her dad. "Uh, Dad? Why do we have to—"

Before she could finish, he'd pulled her out into the rainy night. Her feet sunk into mud up to the laces. She grimaced and groaned, hugging her furry hoody tight around her body as a cold wind blew. She was thoroughly wet by the time they reached the door to the outbuilding.

Inside, it smelled even worse than in the cabin. A little like something had died, a little like poop. She grimaced and looked around, but couldn't see anything. She imagined thousands of spiders, crawling in the darkness.

"Dad," she asked, wondering why he wasn't trying to find a light switch. Maybe there was no electricity in this place. *Probably* there was no electricity. "Aren't you going to find a lamp?"

He didn't answer her. He'd gone to the one window in the place, and was peering out of it. She followed him, shivering, and he put an arm around her.

"Dad," she ventured, after a few moments. "What's a milk house?"

"What do you think, silly? It's where they stored milk," he said, again with that false, too-happy voice.

"Oh," she said. The rain pinged overhead, on the metal roof. It sounded weird, but it was okay because it drowned out her madly beating heart.

It was so hopelessly dark out there, except for the one porch bulb, creating a small halo of light over the guards, standing underneath it. She pressed close to her father and looked out the window, at the two big guards in their FBI tactical gear. They had guns. They'd take care of everything. She was safe. Right?

"Dad," she said softly. "Did Mom send that message?"

He was quiet for a moment. Then he said, "I don't know."

"Do you think she's going to come here?"

"I don't know."

There were so many other questions she had, but what was the use in asking them, if her father didn't know anything? Still, she had to keep trying.

"Dad—"

She froze when she saw something, beyond the rain-spattered windowpane.

It was a split second's flash of movement, nothing more.

As she moved closer to the window, squinting, it happened.

Something, hovering in the shadows outside, sliced into the circle of light, glinting for a beat before disappearing. Kelsey moved even closer, not certain what she'd seen, as the guard closest to them seemed to stiffen, then slowly crumple over, sprawling out on the mud.

She stared, hardly comprehending. Just as it was registering, the slicing motion came again. Something moved in the shadows nearby. The other guard, who'd turned to see what was happening, fell down, too, clutching at his neck.

150

There was a big gash in it, squirting blood between his fingers.

Kelsey opened her mouth to scream.

A hand clamped over her mouth. It was her father.

Too late. The man came into the light, and swung his head in their direction. Then, he started to move purposefully toward their hiding place.

CHAPTER TWENTY SIX

The streets around Lake Kiowa at this time of night were absolutely black and empty. Mia hadn't passed another car in twenty minutes. On a nice night, she'd be able to see the moonlight, reflecting on the still surface of the lake. But this weather was terrible; the rain kept coming, a thick blanket of fog was hugging the road in places, and the wind kept blasting the side of the car, making it shake.

Despite all this, Mia went twice the speed limit, constantly glancing at her phone.

But there was no response. Nothing to signal that they hadn't already succumbed to that madman.

See you at the family reunion.

Her chest burned and her head throbbed as she came to the old Mort's convenience store. It looked as though it had closed down, since there were boards on the windows. Not that it would be open, this late at night. Her headlights streaked across it, and then it was gone, giving way to trees and more trees.

The damn defrost was doing nothing. She reached forward and wiped some condensation from the windshield, squinting as she tried to follow the dotted yellow line in the center of the road.

Her GPS was now spinning, saying *Connection Lost.*

Of course it was. But the entrance to the long driveway to the safe house was around here, somewhere. She knew it.

She tried to slow to a crawl so she could find it, but she was too agitated to take her time. Lurching forward, she knew every moment was of the essence. Somewhere, out there, Kelsey could be in trouble. Each time she thought of her daughter, it sent a sharp spike of worry through her heart, and she pressed on the gas a little more.

Finally, she spotted a narrow break in the trees, and muddy ruts other cars had carved into the path.

She turned onto the drive and fought the urge to gun it, all the way to the house. She had to be careful.

When the light of the cabin came into view beyond the trees, she cut her headlights.

Moving forward slowly, hands gripping the steering wheel, she scanned the area. She could just make out the outline of a blue pick-up truck, among the trees. It was parked off to the side, as if it wanted to remain hidden. As she crawled forward, she took the flashlight from her cell phone and shone it on the truck. It was a nice one, with a small sticker on the door that said, *RENT ME—Jiffy Jerry's,* with a phone number underneath.

Her stomach lurched. It was just as she'd feared. He was here. Somehow, he'd found them.

Moving forward, she continued searching in both directions, looking for any signs of life among the bleak surroundings.

What she saw instead was a sign of death.

There were two lumps, lying motionless on the porch. At first, she willed herself to hope that they were just piles of tactical equipment, but then she saw the face of one of their colleagues, staring up at the sky, unmoving.

She brought a hand to her mouth and swallowed the bile in her throat. She was too late.

No. I can't be. They're still alive, Mia. They're fine, she told herself, stopping the car and pushing open the door.

She stepped out into a mud puddle, and by the time she'd straightened, she was soaked to the skin by the deluge of rain. It blurred everything in front of her. Wiping the drops from her eyes and bracing herself against the wind, she stepped toward the two FBI agents.

Crouching, she checked for a pulse. But there was too much blood, spilling out upon the porch, mingling in the mud puddles. It looked like a scene from a horror movie. They'd each been stabbed in the throat, and stripped of their weapons.

She knew these men. They were rookies, but good men. Strong men. If they could fall to this murderer, what chance did she have?

Carefully stepping over them, she went to the door. There was a dim firelight behind one of the windows, but other than that, it was still and dark. She was just about to turn the doorknob when she heard a cry, to her right.

Kelsey!

She whirled in the direction the sound had come from and rushed toward the side of the house, splashing through the puddles as she forged into the driving rain. A fierce blast of wind off the lake hit her, full-force, as she came around the corner of the house, almost knocking her off balance. Wet ropes of her hair slapped her cheeks, and she shoved them back, straining to see where the sound had come from.

She saw a small white shed, not far away, the red door, banging open and closed in the wind.

Stepping closer, she could've sworn she saw something move inside.

Her hand instinctively went to her side, where she'd have kept her weapon. Again, finding nothing, she felt naked. She looked around for something to use as a weapon. But what could she use? He had the greatest weapon of all—her daughter.

She came to the door just as it was closing again, reached out her hand, and stopped it. Then she stepped inside.

At first, she could see nothing. But as her eyes adjusted to the darkness, she heard a voice.

"The little fly has come to the web. But I already have two more little flies to feast upon."

Slowly, the figures of the three came into view. Aidan and Kelsey, standing together, looking scared to death. Kelsey was trembling. Aidan was stone-faced, but even he was having trouble hiding his apprehension.

And then she focused on her tormentor. The man who had made the past few months of her life a living hell.

It was the man from the photograph. The brother of Wilson Andrews. He was chunkier than the other Andrews, his face a little less movie-star-like, his hair not-quite as full, but they were remarkably similar. He was like the funhouse version of Wilson Andrews, close, but no cigar. He was a man who'd likely spent all of his life in his popular brother's shadow, and wanted to find a way to make his mark on the world.

And he had.

"Jerry Andrews," she said, her voice hollow.

He smiled. "We finally meet, Mia," she said, a sick smile spreading across his face. "After all this time, it's a pleasure."

He sounded just as oily as his brother, every bit the politician. "Why did you do this to me?"

He laughed. "Why did you do this to *me*?" he shot back. "We had everything under control. I'd almost gotten away with it. The media blitz around the girls was finally dying down. The police had given up.

All we had to do was tie up that loose end and get rid of that Little Bird. And then *you* came along. And you ruined everything."

"Your brother—"

"He had very little to do with any of it, really. Of course, he knew. And he didn't want to see his favorite baby brother go to jail. So he did what he had to do to keep my nose clean. And it would've worked . . . " He shook his head. "But again, you were the spider who caught us in your little web. So I decided to catch you in a web of my own."

"What happened to Sara?" she asked, her voice trembling.

He laughed. His hair was wet, his face was red and puffy. Underneath his dark blue windbreaker, she could see what looked like hints of a loud, Hawaiian shirt. He looked like anyone's favorite uncle, really. A big teddy-bear. Harmless. "That's the big puzzle, isn't it? I'm sure you'd like to know that."

He pulled a knife out from behind his back and touched the tip gingerly.

"But I think I'm going to keep that to myself."

She gritted her teeth. "Is she alive?"

He looked at her with disbelief. "Are you kidding me? Why would you even ask me that? Don't you get it . . . all of this, everything I've done, is for her. I love her. She loves me. We're happy together. It's people like you, who don't understand, who insist on ruining things, keeping us apart. If you had just let us alone . . ."

Mia could barely breathe. After all this, *Sara was still alive.*

But as Jerry waved the knife wildly in the air, Mia knew the biggest threat was to her own family.

"All right. We'll leave you alone," she said, holding out her hands in a plea to get him to keep the knife away from Kelsey, who was sobbing quietly.

She needed to do something. Mia had spent all of her life, trying to shield Kelsey from the horrors of the world. And now, here she was, in the hands of a madman. And Mia had delivered her there, herself. If they survived this, would she be the same, happy little girl she'd raised? Or would she be changed forever?

As much as she wanted to save Sara, she couldn't bear the sight of her own daughter, in this kind of pain.

Tears stung Mia's eyes. "Please," she begged.

He studied her, then shook his head slowly. "I don't think so. I don't believe you. You're not the type to give up. You keep coming.

155

That's the reason I knew that when given the chance, you'd break out of prison. You can't leave well enough alone. When there's a thread, you have to pull it."

She shook her head fiercely. "No. That's not true. Give me my daughter, and I swear, I'll leave, and you'll never see me again."

He scowled at her, and the timbre of his voice lowered an octave. "What kind of idiot do you think I am?"

"I swear, I—"

"After all you did to find Sara, I don't think you'd ever leave her so easily."

"I promise. I will."

"No. After all this? I can't let you go that easy. What fun would that be? You like this cat and mouse, don't you? You get off on it. You've been a very worthy adversary. So let's see. What I think is that we should play a little game, instead. You in?"

She shook her head, and opened her mouth to decline.

"I'll give you an option. Either *you're* in, or—" He pointed the knife at Aidan. "*He's* out."

Aidan let out a breath of air and pressed his lips together. He was trying to be strong, but trembling—she could see his resolve cracking. No, he wasn't the type of man who'd beg for his life, but he was as close as she'd ever seen him.

"What do you say, Mia? Want to play a little game?"

She looked at her daughter, with the tears streaming down her face, and all her breath left her. Mia had never wanted anything more than to go to her daughter, console her, wipe away those tears. But again, she was powerless.

She had no choice.

She nodded. "All right."

CHAPTER TWENTY SEVEN

Jerry Andrews paced behind his two hostages, with the easy swagger of a star baseball player heading out to the plate, ready to hit a home run.

"Good," he said, holding the knife in front of him and rubbing his hands together over the handle of it. "I do love a good competition. Here's the deal. In interest of fairness, I'll give you a chance. I'll ask you riddles. For each riddle you get right, you can take a step closer. But each one I stump you on, you have to take a step back. If you reach your family in time, I'll let all three of you go. We'll forget all about this."

She narrowed her eyes at him. Was he insane? He was going to make it that easy? There had to be some catch. He was going to ask impossible questions that had no answer. "What kind of riddles?"

"Just ordinary, everyday riddles," he said with a grin. "I do love my riddles."

Oh, my God, she thought, staring at him in horror. *This has all been just a game to him. This man isn't just a pedophile and a murderer. He's downright insane.*

And in her experience, there was only one way to deal with someone who did not listen to reason., who might fly off the handle at any given moment.

You had to humor them.

"And if I don't get them right?"

"Well, if you make it to the door, then the fly gets to stand there and watch as the spider feasts upon her family."

Kelsey let out a gasp. "Mommy—"

"Shhh, honey. He won't hurt you," Mia whispered, never taking her eyes off the knife. She had no choice. So she said, "Fine. What's the first riddle?"

He stopped and looked up at the ceiling. "We'll start easy. What has an eye but cannot see?"

She hesitated. That was, indeed, easy. She glanced at her husband, trying to determine whether it was truly that simple, or if she was

157

overlooking something. He nodded, almost imperceptibly, and his lips moved.

"Don't help her, you idiot!" Jerry screeched, his face twisting in rage. He grabbed Aidan by the collar and shoved him, head-first, into the wall. His forehead hit it with a sickening crack, and he slumped to the ground, a bright red blotch of blood blooming where he'd made contact.

She gasped, and Kelsey let out a scream.

"Wait," Mia said, holding out her hands. "D-don—"

"Your *answer*?" he demanded.

She couldn't take her eyes off her husband. The blood was rolling down the side of his nose, now. She wanted to go to him, but she was trapped. "A needle."

"Good, good. You may take a step forward," he said brightly, as if he hadn't just beaten up a man.

She thought about taking a giant leap, but she worried that he'd tell her she wasn't playing fair again. She took a normal step. "Next?"

"Don't get impatient, dear," he said, wagging a finger at her. "Let's see . . . here's an interesting one. How high would you have to count before you would use the letter A in the English language spelling of a whole number?"

Her thoughts swam. She couldn't concentrate. Not with Kelsey, sitting there, trembling, begging her to get this right.

She started to count in her head, *one, two, three* . . . and then quickly realized she'd be here forever, so she skipped over numbers and the answer soon came to her. "One . . . thousand."

"Very nice, Agent. I always knew you were a smart one."

Still, Aidan, on his side on the ground, didn't stir. He needed help. An ambulance. She needed to hurry.

She took another step forward, estimating the space between them. Three more questions. Maybe four, and she'd be done. That was, if he held true to his promise. That was a very big "if," considering he was mad. She stared at him, expectant. She was getting impatient to end this, and so close that she could lunge forward and grab that knife from him, if it weren't for her family, standing between them.

"What gets wetter, the more it dries?"

"Towel," she said immediately, taking a step before he'd even given her permission. "Next?"

"Ah, you're good at this, Agent." He spoke slowly, infuriatingly taking his time.

"*Next?*" she prodded. Now, she was resenting him for even putting her in this ridiculous game, making her go through these motions like some puppet on a string.

"What do you call a room with no windows and no doors?" he asked, seemingly unruffled that she was now so much nearer.

"A mushroom," she said at once, taking another step. Just one more.

"All right." He smiled. "If you have a bee in your hand, what's in your eye?"

She hesitated. That was one she hadn't heard. "A . . ." she didn't say more, afraid that if she asked a question, he'd think that was her answer. She looked at her daughter, who was shivering, pleading her mother to get the answer right.

But she didn't know. *Bee in your hand, what's in your eye . . . if you're holding a bee, you're . . .*

It suddenly hit her. "Beauty. Beauty is in the eye of the bee holder."

"Ah, good, I thought I stumped you on that one," he said, as she took another step.

"That's it. I'm here. I did it. Let them go," she said, standing just inches from her family, mere feet from him and his knife.

He laughed and shook his head, just as she'd dreaded. "One more question. And then I'll let them go." He smiled and unzipped his windbreaker. As he did, she looked at his side and noticed he'd tucked one of the revolvers into his pants.

Big mistake. Though movies were fond of showing police officers and criminals doing that, it was never done by anyone competent with a gun, because the risk of something going wrong with that was too great.

That told her one thing. He was probably not skilled with a gun.

She scowled at him. "What's the last question?"

Another big grin. He loved playing with her, didn't he? She felt oily from being played with by him. Her hands were slick, and despite the chill in the air, a trickle of sweat ran down her ribcage. She saw the opening, and decided to grab it in the next moment.

He said, "You have two dogs. How can you give away one and keep bot--"

Before he could finish, she lunged forward, grabbing his hand with the knife. He let out a grunt and tried to shove her off him, but she managed to hold tight to his wrist so he couldn't move it. She twisted the skin there, hard, so that he was forced to drop it, letting it clatter to the floor beside them.

He kicked at her, then grabbed her throat with his other, fleshy hand, shoving her up against the wall.

"Run, Kelsey," Mia managed, fixing her little girl with a stare as the madman began to crush her windpipe.

Kelsey nodded, jumping into action, rushing to the door, toward safety.

"No!" Jerry shouted, as he watched the little girl run off. He turned and focused his wrath on Mia. "You bitch."

The pressure was too much. The air was slowly being forced out of her burning lungs. In another few moments, she'd black out. And she knew this man wouldn't stop until she was dead.

So she reached down, fumbling between them, and found the handle of the gun in his pants. She yanked it out.

Before he knew what was happening, she'd removed the safety and cocked it. She tried to aim it, but his hand swung out, knocking it from her grip.

"No!" she growled out, lunging for it.

Her fingers connected with it just as his weight came down upon her body, making her small frame collapse to the dirt like a house of cards. She tried to grasp the gun, but it was just out of reach. He pulled at her hair, yanking it back so hard, she heard the pop-pop-pop of it, being ripped from her scalp.

Rearing back on her knees, she donkey-kicked backwards, blindly. It connected with his shin. He let out a growl as she propelled herself forward, finally grabbing the gun.

But though she had it in her grasp, as she spun to level it at him, once again, he grabbed her wrist up over her head. His strength was no match for hers. She felt her bones cracking from the pressure, her hand going numb. Soon she'd have to drop the gun.

Their eyes connected. His were wild, full of rage. The man was insane. She thought of her family, now forever changed by this man. Of Sara and Chloe and the countless people whose lives had been ruined.

Somehow, she gathered the strength and pulled up a knee, hitting him squarely in the crotch. He let out a guttural groan, which allowed her to lower the gun. "You bitch!" he bellowed, hands out to grab her as he stalked forward.

The second before she fired, his eyes went wide. The single gunshot rang through the quiet night.

He loosened his grip on her immediately and began to scream. Mia gasped for air as he backed off her, and she saw the bloodstain, blooming across the front of his khaki pants. He looked down, horrified, and started to scream as he realized exactly what had happened.

"I'll kill you!" he shouted, stumbling as he advanced toward her.

"Not if I kill you first." Even if she hadn't been first in firearms training in her class at the Academy, she had this. He was an easy target, and one she had no remorse about firing upon. She held the gun out, taking aim, and pulled the trigger.

She hit him right between the eyes.

"Both," she whispered as he slumped to the ground, his eyes wide with shock. "You name one of the dogs *Both.*"

CHAPTER TWENTY EIGHT

After a moment of stunned silence, where she confirmed the mass at her feet was, indeed, dead, she kicked aside the body and rushed to the other side of the outbuilding, where Aidan was still laying, motionless.

"Aidan," she whispered, rolling him over so she could get a better look at him. She felt a pulse. He was alive, still breathing. "Aidan?"

Nothing.

"Aidan?" She slapped his cheeks a little. "Come on."

To her relief, he let out a moan, and his eyelids fluttered, before he cracked one eye open. "What the hell happened?"

She took him by the collar, and kissed him. "You're going to be okay. I've got to find Kelsey." She stood up and brushed off her jeans, then went to the door. "Kelsey!"

"Right here," a voice that was decidedly *not* Kelsey said. It was male.

A second later, David appeared in the doorway, a frightened Kelsey in his arms, clutching tight to his neck. "What the hell happened?"

She let out a sigh of relief and took her daughter from her partner. "Come here, baby girl." She walked her outside, where the rain had stopped, and now, a sliver of moonlight dodged in and out of the trees and the dark clouds. "Are you all right? It's over now. It's all over."

"Are you okay, Mommy? I was so scared," she said as Mia held her tight, smoothing back her hair.

"Of course. I told you, I wouldn't let anything happen to you."

She smiled and hugged tighter. "And Daddy?"

"I'm here, too," he said, appearing in the doorway.

"Dad!" she shouted, reaching for him, gasping at the sign of his injury. "You're bleeding!"

He wiped at his forehead. "Looks worse than it is, sweetheart."

"Where's that mean man?"

"He's gone," she said, motioning David toward the outbuilding. He went inside, pausing at the door, leaving them alone.

162

They came together in a three-way hug, and Mia let the tears come. This felt so good. It was all she wanted. And yet . . . she knew it couldn't last.

She was still a wanted woman.

When they separated, she walked them away from the horrific scene.

David came out and jogged over to them. "Can I talk to you in private?"

Mia gave Kelsey one last kiss and handed her over to her husband. They walked over to the edge of the tree line, and she said to him, "It was Jerry Andrews. Wilson Andrews's brother. He kidnapped Sara and Chloe, and Wilson knew about it and covered it all up."

He shook his head. "Jesus. That guy is Andrews's brother? And the guy knew his brother was a sick fuck and did nothing about it?"

Mia nodded. "I still don't know where Sara is, but I think she's alive."

He dragged a hand down his face. "All right. We've got a lot of work to do here, to get it all sorted out."

"Thanks, David. For everything."

He shook his head. "I should've believed you when you said what you did about Andrews. I guess—he's a powerful guy. I didn't want to—"

"And I'm sure he'll probably find a way to weasel out of this, get his cronies to cover for him and say he didn't know anything. His brother's dead now, and can't defend himself. But if you do talk to him, do me one last favor?"

David nodded. "Yeah, anything."

"Tell him he can kiss my ass."

David smiled.

They walked back to Kelsey and Aidan, who were standing in the long driveway, near David's SUV, and the blue pick-up. Mia motioned to it. "That's Jerry vehicle."

Kelsey looked at it and blinked. "I've seen that truck before!"

They all turned to stare at her. Mia nodded; it made sense. Jerry had probably been stalking them for a long time, just as he'd stalked Sara. That was how he'd known so much about what Mia was up to. "Where did you see it, baby girl? At home?"

Kelsey shook her head. "At that old store. Just before we got here. The one with all the boards in the window."

At first, Mia thought nothing of it. But then, something registered in her head. "You mean, Mort's?"

Kelsey nodded.

Mia glanced at David, who wrote something down and said, "Got it. We'll check into it."

"Thanks, David."

"You know, you're going to have to get out of here," he said, looking down the road. "I called the police a few minutes ago. I had to. I was worried that--"

"It's all right." She nodded reluctantly, then gazed at her family, trying not to cry. She glanced at the Honda.

"Don't take the car. They're already looking for it," David warned. "You'd be better off going out on foot."

He was right. She couldn't stay with any vehicle for too long. Besides, this place was less populated, meaning less of a chance for her to be recognized. And she'd always liked camping. She could hide out around here, better than anywhere.

"All right." She ran to it and took out her backpack, then hoisted it onto her shoulder, trying to decide where she should go next.

Aidan shook his head in confusion and pointed at the outbuilding. "You don't have to leave. That man in there—"

"No, Aidan. I have to. It doesn't matter. Jerry Andrews might have tried to pin a bunch of crimes on me, crimes which I will hopefully be proven innocent of—"

"I'll do everything I can to make sure that happens," David said.

She smiled gratefully at him, then looked at her husband. "But that doesn't change my original conviction for the murder of Ellis Horvath."

His face fell. "But you didn't do that."

"Speaking of," David said. "I have a little bit of news on that front."

"What's going on?"

He lowered his voice and looked around. "Well, ever since Ellis Horvath was killed, something about that night hasn't set well with me. Then everything you said at the trial . . . about being set up? So I've done a little digging."

"You have?" She was surprised. He was the one who'd called her paranoid, after all.

He rubbed the back of his neck nervously. "Yeah. And you remember Detective Kevin Reynolds at the Dallas Fort Worth PD?"

She nodded. It seemed like ages ago, but he was the man who'd interviewed her after the Ellis Horvath shooting. She remembered that meeting well, because that was the moment when the whole law enforcement world had stopped treating her like a respected member of their ranks and began treating her like a criminal. "What about him?"

"I went back to that factory and started asking questions of the people that lived around there. And it turns out, someone who fits his description was seen skulking about the factory, before Ellis Horvath was shot."

Her eyes widened. "Who told you that?"

He smiled. "Thought you'd ask that." He handed her a paper. "All the info is in here. Name of the witness, phone number. I figured you'd want to look into it."

She took it. "Thank you. I do."

Just then, police sirens began to scream in the far distance. Her heart lurched.

She went to her family, and gave them another three-way-hug. By now, Kelsey was clinging to her as if she was never going to let go, and Aidan had tears in his eyes. He ducked down and kissed her lips. "Mimi. There's got to be some other way—"

"No." She held the paper David had given her, tight in her pocket. "But there is hope. And I'm going to do everything I can to get back to you. I promise."

He nodded. "I know you will."

She kissed him again, then embraced Kelsey, trying her best to commit her daughter's image to memory. She was changing, almost every day. Who knew how different she would look, the next time she saw her?

"I love you," she whispered in her daughter's ear.

Then she turned and headed down the muddy embankment, toward the lake, away from the police cars as they began to close in. Though she wasn't quite sure where she would go, or what she would do next, she knew she would be back in Dallas, her home, soon. She had something to prove, and she would never stop, until she'd done it.

CHAPTER TWENTY NINE

Early that morning, before daybreak, U.S. Marshal Kane Wilcox drove north out of Dallas, into the woods, his rental sedan splashing through puddles from last night's soaking rain.

As he drove, chugging a giant-size commuter coffee from Seven-E, he checked the time on his dash. Precious moments were wasting. He liked to get to the scene of a crime before the blood hit the floor.

But that had proven impossible, with this case. The place was a lot farther out of the way than he was used to, but according to initial reports that had been called in from the FBI, it'd been the scene of one hell of a crime.

He loved those.

He set his big cup in the holder, scrubbed a hand through his graying, bristly hair. He'd last been in the military almost thirty years ago, and he still couldn't picture himself wearing his hair any other way than the high-and-tight.

He'd just started to pull out his cigarettes, when he came upon the circus.

He'd expected this. Somehow, the news always seemed to find out about these things before they did. He passed dozens of news vans on the narrow, winding country road. Police cars and ambulances were everywhere, too. Wilcox got the feeling that this place hadn't seen this much action, ever.

They were all crowded around a broken-down, abandoned convenience store, called Mort's. Supposedly, that missing girl had been found there, after six months. He couldn't blame the place for being a zoo. This was the town's biggest story, ever. Hell, it was probably the *state's* biggest story. The media frenzy that had surrounded that girl's disappearance had been *unreal*.

Wilcox parked his car and navigated through the crowds. Some were press, but others were just neighbors in nightclothes, out to see what the fuss was about. Nudging his way past them and around the old gas pumps, he took in the boarded-up place. There was a sign, rusted and blackened, that said, *Mort's Gas 'n' Go—Your last stop 'til the*

Lake! All of the windows were covered with planks, most of them heavily graffitied. Only the door was open, propped that way by a cinderblock. He could see several police officers, milling about inside.

He flashed his badge to a police officer who looked too young to have the pot belly and be as entirely bald as he was. "What's going on here?"

"Hey, Agent," the officer said, smiling to reveal a missing eye tooth. He shook his hand. "Woo! US Marshals here, too? Nice!"

"Yeah. And you are . . .?"

"Officer Pete Bottoms."

Wilcox nodded curtly, looking around, urging him to give him the answers he was looking for.

"Yeah, uh, come on in," he said, leading him in the front door. The store probably hadn't been open in a few years, at least, judging from the caved-in roof and the condition of the inside.

His eyes went to a pair of handcuffs, one end of them attached to a metal bar near the counter. "Is that where they found the girl?"

"Yeah. So we just rescued Sara Waverly. Sure you heard about her on the news, huh? Kid's good. Doin' well, considering the hell she's been through. The ambulance just left, taking her to the hospital. Can't believe she was right here, chained up in here. Well, seemed like a temporary place, she wasn't always here. I patrol this area a lot, it's my beat, and I never saw nothin'--"

"Who kidnapped her?" he said, cutting the officer off.

"Oh. You want to know that, you gotta go to the other crime scene. Down the road. That's a big mess. Two FBI agents, from what I hear. And the kidnapper. Dead. At least, that's what they're saying. I don't know if--"

"Can you point me in that direction?"

Bottoms nodded and they stepped outside. "Yeah. You go down that road, about a mile. It'll be on your right. Hard to find, usually, but shouldn't be much trouble now, on account of all the commotion going on—"

"What about the escaped convict?"

Bottoms froze, his eyes filling with confusion. "Huh?"

"Agent Mia North. The FBI agent accused of murder. Her family was at the safe house, right? She was here, too?"

He shrugged. "I don't know nothin' about that. Only what I hear on the news. But guess you gotta ask 'em yourself."

Wilcox thanked him and went outside to his car. Sure enough, when he drove to the second crime scene, there were fewer news vans, but a lot more police and official vehicles. He had to park on the main road and walk toward the property, and by the time he got to the old FBI safe house, his cowboy boots were covered in mud.

Again, he flashed his badge to the FBI Agent there, a shorter, well-built African American who was staring off into the distance, looking pissed off at the world. "I'm US Marshal Kane Wilcox. And you are . . ."

The Agent shook his hand and gave him an unimpressed look. It was always like that, between Feds from different agencies. Mostly a dance of who was stepping on whose toes. "David Hunter."

"Hunter." Just as he thought. The name was familiar. Wilcox had spent most of the past few days looking over the Mia North file. He knew that David Hunter, a rookie who'd come onto the force a couple years ago, after two tours in Afghanistan, had been her former partner. He also knew that Hunter had done the unfriendly deed of ratting her out, during the trial that had sentenced her away for a good, long time. From what he'd seen, David Hunter thought his former partner was a little crazy. "What happened here?"

"From what I know," the agent said, motioning to the white outbuilding. "The suspect, Jerry Andrews, brother of Wilson Andrews, the senate hopeful, went after a couple of people being guarded in the safe house."

"A couple of people . . . you mean the family of former FBI Agent Mia North?"

The agent nodded, his eyes narrowed. "That's right."

"Why?"

"He had a vendetta, I guess. Against her. She was the one who'd been trying to nail him for kidnapping Sara Waverly."

"And?"

Hunter shrugged. "And he killed the two agents guarding the house before winding up dead himself."

Wilcox pressed his lips together. "And?"

"And what?"

He stared at this guy, Hunter. Why did he feel like he wasn't being totally straight with him? Trying to keep things from him? "What happened to Jerry Andrews, that he wound up dead?"

Hunter shrugged and looked away. "That, I don't know."

168

"You know Mia North, don't you?" he asked, eyebrow raised.

He nodded. "Yeah. She was my partner," he admitted.

Good boy. At least he has more sense than to lie about that. Because even if I didn't already know, I'd find it out, anyway. Wilcox scanned the area. "The family's here? They're all right?"

Hunter nodded. "Yeah. But . . . I wouldn't talk to them or anything. They're pretty shaken up. Plus, they don't know anything, either."

I sincerely doubt that. He'd had a wife, once. Even loved her, a long, long time ago. But if he were on the run? He'd make damn sure he got in contact with her. That went without saying. "They don't, do they?"

Another shrug. "I just told you. You're wasting your time, talking to them."

Wilcox ran a hand through the bristle of his hair. He'd been in this business a long time. He'd seen the ins and outs of every case, met all kinds of people. But he knew that all Federal Agents were, essentially, like him, in a lot of ways. And if he'd been on the run, another person he'd probably have been in touch with was his partner. That is, if he'd had one. He could smell this kid's bullshit, dripping off of him.

He'd had enough. He crossed his arms. "Listen, kid. Don't dick around with me, or I promise you, there'll be hell to pay. Was Mia North here, or wasn't she?"

Hunter looked at him, and simply shrugged. "Can't tell you."

"Can't? Or won't?"

The FBI agent gave a noncommittal glance in his direction. "Look. I came here this morning because of a call I received from one of my fellow agents. I arrived to find both of them—both of my friends—dead, as well as the victim. So I know as much about all this as you do."

Oh, I sincerely doubt that, Wilcox thought, stepping toward the cabin, navigating through the thick mud, trying to piece together what he could. He saw the dozens of yellow markers, where evidence had been found, and moved carefully around them. He crouched at the front of the house, looking at the muddy footprints, but by now, there were so many of them, all sizes, they could've belonged to anyone. He poked around inside the milk house and asked a few questions, but no one seemed to know exactly what had happened. "Under investigation," they kept saying. "Pending forensic analysis."

Bullshit.

Something stunk here, and Agent Wilcox had a good feeling about what it was.

He milled about in front, watching the other agents accumulating the evidence, going in and out of the main house. He peeked in the cabin window and saw the pretty little girl, Mia North's daughter, and her husband. They made a nice family, but he wasn't here to keep nice families together. That wasn't his job.

His job was to apprehend a wanted escaped convict.

And he was going to do just that.

Especially this one. There was just something so much more interesting about tracking down a fellow federal agent who'd gone rogue. It made it into more of a challenge. A game.

He stepped away from the rest of the crowd and went out to the back of the milk house. There, he found a pair of size seven female footprints. Undisturbed. They looked fresh, heading off in the direction of the lake.

He followed them down to the water's edge, where they turned east, and kept on going.

So would he. As long as it took.

That was why he had his reputation. He *always* pinned his quarry.

He smiled. He loved this part of the job. *Agent North,* he thought, dragging the damp lake air into his lungs. The sun was just breaking over the hills in the distance, a new day was dawning, and he felt like a bloodhound that had just caught its target's scent. *Bring it on, Agent North. The game is afoot.*

NOW AVAILABLE!

SEE HER HIDE
(A Mia North FBI Suspense Thriller—Book 2)

Fugitive FBI Agent Mia North knows that hunting down killers and solving new—and old—cases is the only way to clear her name. When a rash of high-school girls are found murdered, discovered on the soccer field, the case is personal for Mia. Can she find and stop the killer—and figure out who framed her—before she is caught by the U.S. Marshals?

In SEE HER HIDE (A Mia North FBI Suspense Thriller—Book Two), Special Agent Mia North is a rising star in the FBI—until, in an elaborate setup, she's framed for murder and sentenced to prison. When a lucky break allows her to escape, Mia finds herself a fugitive, on the run and on the wrong side of the law for the first time in her life. She can't see her young daughter—and she has no hope of returning to her former life.

The only way to get her life back, she realizes, is to hunt down whoever framed her.

Mia's former partner desperately needs her help: high-school soccer players are turning up dead in neighboring towns, with no rhyme or reason. Mia may be the only one who can solve it.

But her position is tenuous and she has no one to back her up.

Might she, working alone and racing against the clock, stumble right into the killer's hands?

An action-packed page-turner, the MIA NORTH series is a riveting crime thriller, jammed with suspense, surprises, and twists and turns that you won't see coming. Fall in love with this brilliant new female protagonist and you'll be turning pages late into the night.

Book #3 in the series—SEE HER SCREAM—is now also available.

Rylie Dark

Debut author Rylie Dark is author of the SADIE PRICE FBI SUSPENSE THRILLER series, comprising three books (and counting); the MIA NORTH FBI SUSPENSE THRILLER series, comprising three books (and counting); and the CARLY SEE FBI SUSPENSE THRILLER, comprising three books (and counting).

An avid reader and lifelong fan of the mystery and thriller genres, Rylie loves to hear from you, so please feel free to visit www.ryliedark.com to learn more and stay in touch.

CPSIA information can be obtained
at www.ICGtesting.com
Printed in the USA
BVHW031641040122
625447BV00028B/2